Neighbors

Joan
Leslie
Woodruff

Third Woman Press
Berkeley

This book would not have been possible without the support of the Ethnic Studies Department at the University of California, Berkeley.

Copyright © 1993 by Joan Leslie Woodruff

Zuni ceremonial translations reprinted by permission from the Smithsonian Institution Press from "A Theology of the Earth," by René Dubos, in *U.S. Bureau of American Ethnology Annual Report 1929–30*.

Typeset by The Typesetting Shop, Oakland, Calif.
Printed and bound by McNaughton & Gunn, Saline, Mich.

Address inquiries to: Third Woman Press, Ethnic Studies, Dwinelle Hall 3412, University of California, Berkeley, CA 94720.

First published 1993

93 94 95 96 97 12 11 10 9 8 7 6 5 4 3 2 1

Library of Congress Cataloging-in-Publication Data

Woodruff, Joan Leslie, 1953–
    Neighbors / Joan Leslie Woodruff
      p.   cm.
    ISBN 0-943219-08-6 : $11.95
    1. Indians of North America — New Mexico —
    Fiction.   I. Title
PS3573.06264N45   1993   92-42761
813'.54—dc20   CIP

1

I thought I would be living there until my feet turned skyward and some generic coroner tied a tag to my toe. Then a miracle happened. It occurred to me I didn't have to live there; it had all been a misunderstanding. For thirty-nine years I had believed I was attached to Los Angeles—physically. I was raised there, and my brain had come up with the idea we were connected by an umbilical cord from hell.

Then, on a rare day when I could see the sky and mountains peering down upon my basin metropolis, I lost it. "Went out of control," the policeman who eventually subdued me said. Two of my neighbors, nameless to me though I'd lived next door to them for thirteen years, assisted the uniformed protector of mankind while he handcuffed me to his squad car. I waited, a collared criminal leashed to her captor's trusty steed, until the policeman's backup arrived.

"What'd she do?" the backup asked.

I struggled and strained against the bracelets that bound me until I could eye the first officer while he responded. "Her neighbors," he gestured to the obese woman with curlers in her hair and the bodybuilding golden boy who stood on the sidewalk in front of my house, "put in a 911 on her. When I got here she was standing on her roof waving a pair of scissors around, screaming at the sky."

"What about?"

"Not sure. She kept saying she'd cut the cord, things like that."

"Wild. Know anything else about her?"

"Her neighbors here," he gestured again, "said she's some kind of nurse. Works over at Memorial Hospital."

I wasn't a nurse, but I'd let them find that out themselves.

"Think she's on drugs?"

"Could be."

I'd never taken drugs of any kind. They were going to spend a lot of taxpayer's money to know that one too, because I'd already decided not to talk. It'd taken me all my life to realize what I'd realized, and I wasn't going to share the secret. They could grow old and die in L.A., but I was getting out.

My exit was extended two weeks longer than I'd intended. The policemen 5150'd me into the psychiatric ward of the county hospital. There are fates worse than death by torture. Two weeks in that facility is one of them.

During one of the ward's interdisciplinary meetings, the shrink-coat assigned to me told a room full of staff—not the infectious kind, but similar in character—that I was experiencing a breakdown of my defense mechanisms.

Defense mechanisms? I obsessed on that thought. Defense mechanisms, as in white blood cells, ready to gobble up staph, or staff, whatever was handy. I liked the idea and must have let it show, because the shrink stopped talking. I looked round the table and noticed they were all watching me. My mouth was turned up in a silly grin.

"She seems to be having a hallucination," shrink finally said. All heads nodded.

I kept my silence and let them play their game. I knew the game. My hospital insurance had a limit for time spent in psyche facilities: fifteen days, if spent consecutively. On day fifteen, I was declared "stabilized, no longer a threat to self or society," and released. I packed my few belongings, adding tissue, hand lotion, shampoo, toothpaste, slippers—the things they'd supplied me with—and was escorted out through the emergency room by a social worker.

I was almost to the door when one of the ER crew recognized me. "Dana Whitehawk? Dana? That you?"

Inches from a clean getaway, and spotted! "Yes."

"You know her?" the social worker asked.

"Sure," the ER nurse replied. "She's the head dietitian over at Memorial."

"You are?" the social worker turned betrayed eyes upon me.

"You been a patient here?" the ER nurse asked, ignoring the social worker's surprise.

"Yeah."

"You didn't like the doctors at Memorial?"

"Didn't get a choice," I smiled.

The nurse glanced at the social worker, who desperately wanted to break his oath of patient confidentiality, tell her where I'd been, how difficult I'd been. His oath won out and he said nothing.

"Nice seeing you," I said in parting, then walked through the heavy double doors to freedom.

Well, almost freedom. I still had to get out of L.A.

Life hadn't been easy for me. I was born on the Choctaw Reservation near Philadelphia, Mississippi, and mailed to Los Angeles while still an infant, to be adopted by a late middle-aged couple who died of old age just after I graduated from high school. I didn't know much about my birth parents, except my mother's name was Whitehawk—which I legally assumed when I found out —and I was of American Indian origin. I occasionally wondered if I was Choctaw, or just a diluted blend of ketchup.

Still, I always enjoyed telling people I was a native original— that I didn't know squat about native culture I always failed to mention. But I knew my brain was different than those I grew up around. I had a viewpoint entirely my own, and my perceptions of people or the world never resembled anyone else's. That is why, when the policeman thought I'd lost control, I believed I'd finally found it; and when the shrink thought my defense mechanisms were askew, I wasn't trying to defend myself against anything— for a change. I was doing the opposite. I was opening up, a late blooming flower, ready to free my soul from a place that'd always been like a prison.

I left the hospital that morning and walked home. Five miles. There, I packed my suitcases and left a note for my landlord which read: I'm gone.

Next, I phoned Memorial Hospital, said I wasn't coming back, withdrew my money from the bank, then with my all-American Honda, set out across California. Out of California. Into Arizona. I didn't like Arizona. On to New Mexico. New Mexico I liked.

I bought a house in the mountains north of Santa Fe from Sam Hoskins, a decayed old cowboy. Now there was a man who should've had a tag on his toe decades ago. "You a painter, or one of them artist types?" he asked while I signed the deed and title transfer papers.

"No."

"Get a lot of them artist types in these parts."

I shrugged. If I had an artistic talent, it was a well kept secret from me.

"You gonna get a job in Santa Fe?"

I shrugged again. The house was older than Sam the fossil, needed plenty of repairs, and included forty acres of land. In California it would've cost a bundle. I paid cash and had money left in my savings, which wasn't big to begin with. But I estimated I could live frugally for one or two years before I had to beat the pavement in search of a job.

"Young woman like you'll probably hook herself a man anyway," he said.

I looked across the table. I didn't consider myself young, yet in comparison to him I figured the Mona Lisa was young. As for hooking a man, I simply didn't believe one existed who was good enough. I shook my head at his suggestion, scribbled name and date on the last form, and handed the papers to the escrow agent. She scanned through them, was satisfied, and finished the transaction by saying, "Congratulations, and welcome to New Mexico." I thanked her, nodded at the fossil, and went out to the parking lot where some kid was studying my hubcaps.

"You desperate, or what?" I asked. A seven-year-old Honda is not a BMW. He spun around, then raced off. While I was adjusting my sun-glasses and inserting key into ignition, the old cowboy appeared at my window. I rolled it down.

"Hope you like your neighbors," he said.

I stared at him. The forty acres was isolated. Besides my house, no other structures existed as far as the eye could see, unless a very old pueblo-in-ruins and two long abandoned adobes counted as structures. "Sure," I said, "I'll love 'em." I guessed his comment was a joke, so I winked, set my transmission, and left the parking lot.

2

Turquoise Teepee was the name of the motel where I'd holed up until the sale was completed. Teepee. That's how it was spelled on the sign. I was hardly a scholar of language, but I didn't think the Sioux or Dakota spelled it that way, tipi being one of their words.

It was late afternoon before I was ready to leave Santa Fe. I loaded my belongings out of room 2-A at the old Turq-Tee, visited a grocery store, a hardware, and a Sears, then headed northwest towards Pojoaqua Valley and Nambe. My new home was situated near these towns, which were little more than names on a map since I'd yet to visit either.

While I drove I found myself awestruck by my surroundings. A few inches of autumn snow made stubborn stake-outs on the shady slopes of canyons and hills; a sleepy calmness settled across the rest of the land's carpet of pale winter grass where juniper, cedar and piñon greenery competed with the gold, red, and brown of aspen and cottonwood. Yet nothing could compete with the wildlife.

These emerged from dens or hiding places and stood cautiously near the edge of the two-lane highway. My first delight was a herd of fragile looking beige-colored deer who paused to graze at the banks of a half-frozen river. Rabbits were abundant, seeming to pop up from nowhere, hopping off similarly—with an occasional coyote in pursuit. Once a fat silky skunk scuttled out from a bush and was nearly hit by a car approaching in the opposite lane. But the driver slowed, and the lovely animal escaped, his disagreeable fume-factory intact.

I cast a glance skyward in time to sight something magnificent and graceful, something I'd never seen outside of pictures: a bald eagle in flight. My heartbeat quickened and I imagined I was having what the California-Cool (a category excluding me) nonchalantly refer to as "an out of body" experience. When I first spotted the eagle I pulled the Honda over and got out. It's massive wings stroked the sky, painting a shadow of its shape upon the ground. While I watched it coast with the wind, I felt myself rising up to meet it. For a brief time I sensed we soared together above the earth—friends in spirit. So absorbed I was I forgot my physical self, which tripped over a rock and fell down a short embankment, scratching knees and ripping jeans.

While I climbed up the bank a couple of cars slowed and people viewed me with amusement, then drove on. I brushed loose dirt from my clothes and hair, decided to leave out-of-body experiences to the exclusive group, and resumed my travels.

It was almost dusk when I reached the turn-off, but light enough I could make out the area. Things were as I remembered; there were no other lived-in structures anywhere near, negating Sam the fossil's comments about neighbors.

A county maintained dirt road bordered one side of my property, following the tree-lined barbed wire fence. The fence continued beyond the road creating a boundary on the east side, and stretched approximately one-half mile, ending at the gate entry. My house sat on a rise a hundred yards from the gate, at the end of a poorly kept gravel driveway. My view to the north was of a hilly pasture which dropped into a small valley. In the distant north, huge mountain peaks pierced the clouds, and all around me an assortment of evergreen trees densely dotted the earth. Most were bushy junipers, branches heavy with blue-colored berries. Next in abundance were large, fat salt cedars, looking like picnickers feasting across every visible slope. Last, and most majestic, were piñon pines of modest height, their slender trunks supporting full crowns of pine boughs and cones.

I focused now on the yard. There was no garage, only a hard-packed clay area at the rear of the house. Heavy gray-black clouds were moving in from the southwest, hinting snow. Fine with me. I was eager to try my hand at putting fires in my fireplace. I'd never had a real fireplace before, and wondered if there would be cut wood around somewhere. I couldn't remember seeing any the day the fossil showed me the property.

The house was a brown, plastered adobe, badly in need of new plaster. I hoped a fresh coat of paint would suffice because I didn't have a clue how to apply plaster. I dug out my key, opened the screen, and started to unlock the door. It wasn't necessary since the door was already open. Cautiously I pushed it wide and reached in, flipped the light switch on. The small scarred mahogany dining room table (the house came furnished) sparkled, and appeared to recently have had a polish. The white vinyl floor was sparkling, too. I threw my handbag on the table and passed to the right into the old fashioned kitchen. The counter top was white tile, the cabinets and drawers were hardwood with a thick coat of yellow paint. I'd been too pleased with the price I was paying, and noticed little about the house. But I remembered the rusted sink. This was a new sink: stainless steel with two deep tubs and a fancy new faucet. Sam the fossil must've removed the rusted one within the last day or two and installed this. I turned round, opened the refrigerator, was surprised to find it cold, a dozen fresh eggs its only occupant. I dropped the fossil part and decided Sam was a nice fellow. He'd cleaned—or hired someone to clean—the house, and left me eggs.

It was odd, the eggs, because I'd bought groceries and only just remembered when I drove up that I'd forgot eggs.

A dark narrow hallway separated the kitchen from the bathroom. The hallway turned a corner to open on two large bedrooms at the right, a spacious living room at the left. Both bedrooms had beautiful polished cedar floors. The living room and hallway had old blue carpet, which would have to go. It was awful.

I flipped the lights on in the bedrooms. No furniture. Sam told me the bedroom furniture wasn't worth keeping. Guess he threw it out. What would I sleep on? I had a good sleeping bag, which would have to suffice until I could get back into Santa Fe.

Each bedroom had one medium size window, the living room had two large windows, and the dining room had two small windows. None had shades or drapes. I had my portable sewing machine so this wasn't a problem. Besides, I had to paint the entire house, inside and out, and drapes would've had to come down.

While I browsed through each room, I made mental notes about necessary repairs and materials I needed to purchase. Afterward I hauled in my possessions and spliced my portable color television into the hook-up in the living room. Sam said there was an antenna for the television and radio. Before I settled down to see how it worked, I stocked my cupboards and refrigerator, hung towels in the bathroom, and stacked bed linen in the hall closet.

I started in to try the television, changed my mind, and scrambled a couple of the gift eggs. I perked half a pot of coffee, toasted a slice of bread, then settled myself comfortably at my dining room table. A calmness seemed to be moving into my soul much the way I was moving into the house. Contentment I think, but I'd never been content in my life, and I couldn't be sure.

When my stomach was satisfied, I decided to test my bathtub. It was strange, but I liked it. It was heavy cast iron, coated with ivory colored porcelain, balanced on sturdy iron claws. I soaked till my skin wrinkled, donned my nightgown, and finished the evening lounging in my sleeping bag while watching farm reports. The farm channel is the only one I could get clear reception on. Before falling asleep I added "adjust the outside antenna" to my list of chores.

Next morning I awoke to sounds of a rooster crowing. I sat bolt upright in the sleeping bag and wondered if there were such things as wild chickens. If not, who owned the rooster and why did it sound so close by?

The fossil—ah, Sam, had said, "Hope you like your neighbors." Maybe he meant I had chickens for neighbors. I got out of my sleeping clothes, into a sweater and jeans, and set out to meet these clucking characters.

A few seconds of morning air sent me scurrying back for a jacket, warm gloves and heavier socks. Snow hadn't fallen, but the ground was frozen hard and my breath came out in dense clouds of steam.

When properly attired, I reset myself to following the rooster's crowing. My house was made private from highway traffic by dozens of trees from the evergreen family. The trees were twenty, thirty, and forty feet high, with dense growth to ground level. I wandered amongst them briefly and decided it was too cold for chickens. Then I remembered the abandoned adobes. I shook my head. They were in the wrong direction, being east of the county road. The crowing came from the west.

"Aha!" I thought aloud, "There are chickens living in the old pueblo!"

I hiked up and down hilly terrain until I was beyond the west boundary of my acreage. I spotted him right away. The rooster was a large red and black creature. He was perched on the highest wall of the ancient pueblo ruins, which butted up into the cliffside of a rocky hill. When the rooster saw me he flew into a courtyard-type area, joining six, seven, maybe eight hens. From the higher ground where I stood it was difficult to know how many chickens there were total. Part of the rock-adobe wall concealed a third of the courtyard.

It was the first time I'd ventured near the pueblo. Sam told me about it, but I hadn't been interested at the time. I vaguely recalled it was between four and nine hundred years old. He said it'd belonged to a small village of Pueblo Indians, but I knew better than that. History was my favorite subject, especially history about the European invasion of North America. If the ruins were more than five hundred years old, they weren't Pueblo Indians. I don't know who they were. Pueblo is a Spanish word. The Spaniards changed a lot of Indian people's tribal names to fit more with their own culture, the same way they built Catholic missions on top of kivas. The Spaniards thought it was pagan the way Indians prayed to kachinas. They erected clay "Mother Marys" and "patron saints-this-and-that" instead, then beat the Indians until they learned to pretend to worship clay. Ironic thing was, Indians didn't actually pray to kachinas in the first place. I think it was a case of cultural misunderstanding on the part of the Spaniards—or maybe intolerance? Not having a religion of my own, I didn't often preoccupy myself worrying about other people's gods.

While I stood there studying the pueblo, I decided Sam was right with both his guesses. It was four hundred years old, and it was nine hundred years old. For a moment I almost thought I saw them—the people who'd lived there for so many centuries.

3

I was searching for a safe way to get to the pueblo when I discovered a type of stairway made out of brick-hard clay and flat rocks. The steps were approximately five feet wide and three feet deep, with short rises of not more than two inches. They appeared to have been there, snuggled next to the rocky hillside which towered above the pueblo, for eons. Maybe not eons. Probably only as long as the pueblo.

Still, this was very impressive. I knelt down, ran my hand over the frozen clay, marveled at the architectural genius of whoever designed it. Not only had it endured a harsh land known for devil winds, black ice, and relentless scorching sun, but it was very functional. The width and shallowness of the steps made it convenient for elderly people with diseased joints to climb the hill with minimal effort. It also made safe travel for someone carrying heavy loads. I wondered about such people. It was a simple thing, the stairway, but it spoke volumes. For the first time in my life I felt close to a group, this group long-dead, because they had cared about their own.

Sentimental thoughts like that embarrassed me and I felt my face go red, felt glad no one was there to catch me in this rush of mush. Then I laughed. The situation was typical for me, the person who found it impossible to share bonds with anyone or anything—living. I laughed again, lost my footing, and ended up sitting two steps below where I'd started.

I quickly discovered frozen ground is very slippery. I steadied myself to avoid tumbling the rest the way, and carefully placed one foot before the other, holding the rock ledge at my left as I descended.

The stairway circled round the cliff, depositing me at the side of a mud wall which blended, in material and color, with the terrain and caused me to think of camouflaged military compounds. I was sure these people had something similar in mind.

I left the cold morning shade of the wall and entered the sunny courtyard, where Rooster and his Happy Hens picked and pecked greedily at grain which had been sprinkled by generous hands across a white frost-covered ground. Peculiar. Who'd brought the grain? I took slow steps towards the feeding chickens, noticed how my shoes left imprints in the frost. I looked behind, saw my own tracks, saw scratches made by chicken feet. I surveyed the yard. It was large, about one hundred feet by one hundred feet, and it was walled in by adobe bricks on three sides, with the pueblo making up the fourth boundary.

"The only way..." I thought aloud, going toward the single opening in the pueblo. But when I was inside, things were even more confusing. A fifty pound burlap bag leaned against dark walls in one corner. It was tied shut with a piece of white rope— new rope. I untied it and found what I'd expected. Chicken grain. A coffee can lay on top of the grain, probably used for a scoop. There was no frost here, just a heavy layer of soft sand which appeared to have been accumulating for a century. I looked round and saw nothing to indicate human presence in the room except for my own tracks, easy to see in this sand.

A small shadow watched me now from the door hole. I say hole because it was probably never a defined doorway, more like a wide crack, having caved in a bit at the sides and top. Still, the whole place seemed in remarkable condition. I looked over without moving my head to see what created the shadow. It was Rooster. He cocked his head from side to side, studying me, probably as curious about me as I was about who took care of him and his Happy Hens.

At that moment the sun sent a spray of light through what was left of the floor overhead. The room, no longer cloaked in darkness, revealed cracks and holes in all the walls. On the left side of the room was another doorway-hole, which I passed through, forgetting Rooster. Hearing noises behind me, I noticed he hadn't forgotten me. He was following, watching.

This room had similar dimensions as the first, but was in better repair. Instead of a sand floor, this had straw...and horse droppings! Granted, they weren't fresh, but it was proof a horse had been using the pueblo in the recent past. Sam said he had owned no livestock for years. I wondered if the horse was wild, or perhaps someone used this property for grazing. I shrugged, decided as long as they didn't live too close by, I didn't care if other people used the property. Didn't belong to me, anyway. Nothing I could say or do if it was being grazed, but there was the problem of a fence. A fence didn't exist between my property and this acreage. Too soon to make a problem where one wasn't apparent, at least not present-time apparent.

I crawled through another opening in the rear wall and found myself standing in a very dark, narrow corridor made tunnel-like by the debris. The floor above seemed more intact, because no light stripped the blackness but for the bit that followed me from the horse room. Rooster flew onto the ledge of the crack from the horse room but made no effort to follow me into this black hole. I considered going home to fetch the flashlight from my Honda, but didn't want to give up a moment of this interesting expedition. Besides, it was too cold for snakes or spiders, and I could think of nothing else I wasn't willing to confront.

Using both hands extended out front and to my sides, I inched through the tunnel. Frequently my toes encountered obstacles, which I stepped across, or crawled over. My adrenaline began pumping buckets of energy and my blood pushed excitement through my body like a runaway train. I wanted to scream, I liked what I was doing so intensely. I wasn't sure *what* I was doing, but it was leaps and bounds above anything I had ever done before. Suddenly something occurred to me.

"What if these things I'm stepping on are skeletons," I called back to Rooster. He crooked his neck and strained his eyes to locate me, but I think he must've decided I was a loony-bird, not deserving his sympathy if I did fall amongst dead bodies. I stooped to run my fingers over one of the things I had tripped on; it was a pile of dusty adobe mud. Before I removed my hand I touched something smooth and very cold. I grasped it, lifted it to my eyes. It was a potsherd, and I could make out a geometric design, part of a decoration on the bowl or vessel the piece came from. I pocketed it in my jacket, and continued my journey.

A few yards farther and I was rounding a corner. I knew what was on the other side of the wall to my right: open land. I'd traveled past the length of the courtyard by now, and was moving toward deeper sections of the pueblo. I was about to give up finding a route into the rooms beyond the wall to my left when my hand met with a draft of air, then a door or window, which I almost fell through.

This room was tiny and cluttered with ancient baskets and more adobe debris. I realized that what I was looking at was visible because the room beyond this was sprayed with sunlight. Where a narrow door had once joined these areas, only a wide space remained near the top half. I climbed up and wiggled through, thankful for being tall and slender. A larger person could never explore these ruins without further damaging these walls in order to create accessible passage. I was overcome with an intense desire to own the pueblo, make it my private playhouse, prevent it from ever being changed.

Suddenly an image grew large in my mind. I saw myself attached to this pueblo, connected by the umbilical cord from hell. I shook my head until the picture vanished, decided I didn't really want to possess the place. What I wanted was to make sure no one else possessed it, either.

I thought of the horse droppings, and Rooster, and the Happy Hens. Animals I didn't resent. Animals could live anywhere they chose, and I was content, always, to have them around, satisfied with their right to be free. Still, something wasn't right.

I thought aloud, "Who has been keeping these animals here? That would have to be a person, and I don't want people in this pueblo! I'll feed the chickens, and I'll feed the horse, if it comes back." It was something I could worry about later.

The room I was now in was cleaner than the others. It was about ten feet by ten feet, and had shelves molded into all the walls. The floor was hard red clay with a round hole in the middle of it. I went to it, knelt down, and found it was a deep hole, black with the stain of burned coal, probably from centuries of fires to keep the room warm. Or cook food. Or bake clay pottery. My knowledge of pueblos was limited to historical data. I didn't recall having read about a room like this.

I sat on the ledge created by what remained of one of the shelves. My eyes lifted upward, and I noticed for the first time that the rooms above were scattered. They weren't all together, crowded, like a hotel. Directly above me a line of rooms formed a boundary around what'd once been an open place similar to the courtyard outside. Most of these were in ruin too advanced to explore without risk of falling through a floor, but if I was careful I believed I could get a closer look.

The ledge I was seated on gave me a boost and I wedged my toes into the walls, heaved myself onto what remained of the roof. From this new vantage point I had my first true perspective of the pueblo. Knowing what I already did about the average room size, the circling corridor, and the scattered layering of second and third story floors, I guessed the original structure had between forty and fifty rooms. In its current state, there were only two actual third story rooms, and these had only partial walls. The top halves of the rooms were entirely gone, leaving them like huge chimney stacks with windows.

Buttress-like appendages emerged from most of the walls, suggesting locations of rooms which had long ago crumbled, became dust, and blew off with the winds to settle on distant sites. I was selective about where I placed my feet while I stretched and pulled myself over and through the second level. I wasn't looking for anything and wouldn't have had a clue what to look for, when I spotted three huge domes on the ground outside the pueblo. They resembled gigantic mud mushrooms which might have sprouted from the soil. I was so distracted by them, I nearly took a tumble through the roof. Regaining my balance, I located a hole large enough to slip through, then lowered myself till my feet met with a pile of adobe.

Once back on the ground, I discovered it was not easy getting out. The rooms became a confusion of darkness, dusty and cold, cluttered full of debris which greatly impeded my escape. I crawled through wall cracks, wiggled through windows and the remains of doorways, and often found myself in rooms I'd already seen. If I were inclined to hysterics, I might have succumbed to a tantrum complete with hyperventilation and fainting. I hate hysterical people. The chaos and confusion was a game I believed the pueblo played to force a tighter bond between it and myself. After a time the game turned simple, and I began to understand the entire structure. I had it memorized, room to room, encircling corridors, areas with storage shelves, fire holes, and exit pathways. I'd even located a bonus, a kind of secret tunnel which dropped from a corner room at the back of the structure, ran the distance of the pueblo's northern-most side, and emerged just beyond an outside wall near where the mud domes sat.

With frozen knees and feet, I crawled out of the passageway, brushed myself off and began to stomp my feet to thaw my toes. This commotion startled a deer grazing on the grass which surrounded the domes. While I watched the creature dart up the hill and vanish among the trees, I wondered about the purpose for such a tunnel. Even more amazing was the fact that such a thing still existed. It'd been carved from the hard-clay soil, was approximately three feet wide and three feet tall, and showed no tactile signs of decay or cave-in. I say tactile, because once inside I couldn't see anything. I had to feel my way along. I'm not sure why I dropped myself into the thing—a dangerous action. But I sensed it was safe and somehow knew where it would deposit me.

When my limbs thawed I turned my attention to the domes. These were not mysterious. All three were practically identical in dimension, and stood in a row facing the pueblo. They were ovens. I imagined they were used to bake food and turn green clay into finished pottery. I was familiar with the baking process of ceramics and clays, and marveled at these designs. After a close examination, I was excited to find one oven was still in remarkable condition. I decided to add a few pounds of clay to my shopping list.

Without a doubt, I loved this pueblo.

4

I was thinking how good a cup of hot coffee would be when a foreboding shadow appeared overhead. I gazed up to see a storm pushing what was left of the morning sun eastward. Dense gray-black clouds, similar to the ones I'd seen the evening before, were rolling in. These definitely meant snow. Already flakes as large as a quarter were blowing across the frozen land. Holding my jacket, which was fast becoming insufficient protection from this biting chill, I started home.

After ascending the cliff stairway I thought about the chickens. Would they be okay? I told myself they were used to this weather, it was their weather, their home. Then it occurred to me, I hadn't seen a watering dish. Where did they get their water? Had to be from the spring I'd seen near the cliff top. A strand of ice emerged from a crack in the red rock, delivering frozen water down a shallow ditch at the cliff-side. Watching the snow spit a steady pattern of white, burying the frozen spring, I knew Rooster and his Happy Hens wouldn't be having a drink any time soon. I hurried to my kitchen, found a metal washing tub beneath the sink, half filled it with scalding water, and hauled it back to the pueblo.

The chickens were roosting—in the straw room with horse droppings—on ancient pine timbers which jutted out from the crumbling walls. I set the tub on the ground and tested it with my finger. The temperature had already dropped to lukewarm. "Get yourselves a good swig of this now," I said, "or it'll be a block of ice." Rooster crooked his neck and eyed me curiously, the way he had when I disappeared down the pitch-black corridor, but none of my feathered friends stirred from their perch. It was the best I could do. By now I was dreaming of that hot cup of coffee, so I set my sights toward home.

By the time I reached my door, the earth was blanketed in bright sparkling snow, from the Sangre de Cristo's in the east to the Jemez peaks in the west. Beautiful. Truly beautiful.

My furnace was powered by butane, stored in a two hundred gallon tank located near the back door, midway between the house and driveway. When I bought the house I didn't think to inquire how much fuel was in the tank. None! This was a bad time to discover the tank was empty. What little was left in the lines, I'd used up during the night.

"Fine mess, Dana old gal," I grumbled. One look out the window told me I wasn't driving anywhere this day, or for several days. The Honda didn't have snow tires, or chains, and I was too inexperienced with bad weather driving to tackle it unarmed.

The question remained: What would I use to stay warm? There was a building Sam called his workshop, located a few dozen yards from the back door. Maybe it contained dry firewood. At that moment wet firewood would suffice. I traded the jacket for a heavy coat and dry gloves, and made my way to the workshop. It was locked. "Damn!" I knew Sam hadn't provided the key. He'd issued me one key, the one for the house, and I wasn't sure that one worked, since my door was ajar when I arrived.

My mind began to obsess about these things. Peculiar. The door had been open, it was freezing outside, and yet the house was toasty warm, as if someone had just been there, turned on the furnace, forgot to pull the door completely shut. And what about the eggs? Fresh, a full dozen. I remember taking two out to scramble, and now that I thought about that, they felt warm, couldn't have been in the refrigerator very long.

I'd dismissed the mystery, thinking it was Sam. Now I remembered, Sam said he was staying with his son in Santa Fe when we finished our escrow business. Sam drove a full-size GMC truck with heavy all-weather tires. Tires like that would've left tracks in my driveway. There weren't any tracks.

Then there were the chickens, pecking away at breakfast. Someone had to untie the feed sack, carry a can of grain to the courtyard, sprinkle it around, replace the can, and retie the sack. But who could do that without leaving footprints?

"Neighbors!" I thought loudly. Had to be the neighbors Sam

was talking about. "Where are these people?" I asked, "and why don't they leave footprints?"

It was all very interesting, but I was freezing and my house wasn't getting any warmer. I started to cross my yard when I noticed the television antenna. I trekked through the snow, around the house, noting that it extended from the roof directly above my living room. I thought, "If I had a ladder..."

My eyes caught something. It was a type of conduit, anchored in concrete. It carried a pole up the side of the house and poked through the overhang of roof. The antenna! I could adjust it by loosening the joints in that conduit and repositioning the direction of the pole.

I hurried to the Honda, dug through my emergency tool box, and found vice-grips and wrench. Then I went inside to turn the television on so I could watch through the open door and see what happened when I moved the pole.

After about an hour I had early stages of frostbite on all fingers and toes, and perfect reception on two major network stations. I put my tools away and ran a bathtub full of very hot water. Thank goodness my water heater and most of the major appliances were electric.

I soaked in the tub until my circulation was restored, after which I jumped out, dried in record time, and donned layers of warm clothes. A few minutes later I was nestled in my sleeping bag, watching an old movie on television. That's when I first saw the firewood. It was stacked neatly in a large wood bin beside the hearth. I stared at it for a few minutes, trying to decide if it was really there. I was positive my hearth had been empty earlier. I'd looked in the wood bin. Not even a splinter of kindling.

What in the world was going on? Perhaps that shrink-coat wasn't as wrong as I'd believed. Maybe I was hallucinating, and none of these things existed in the real world. I crawled from the sleeping bag, went to the kitchen, took one of the gift eggs out, and dropped it. It smashed across my clean linoleum floor. I knelt down, put my hand in the mess, pulled it back, watched yellow yolk ooze from my fingers.

No hallucinations here. The egg was very real; meant the chickens had to be real; and the firewood; and someone was coming down my driveway.

Looking through curtain-less windows, I recognized Sam's

pickup. It was huge and heavy, and negotiated deep snow with the ease a cat negotiates a climb up a tree. I was eager to blast him about the butane tank's empty status, but resented the invasion of my new-found privacy. Grumbling, I loosely stacked two pieces of the mystery wood into my corner adobe-dome fireplace, crumpled a section of yellowed newspaper between the wood, and lit a match. The flames caught immediately. By the time I heard snow crunching under Sam's shoes, a blazing warmth pulsed beyond the red tiled hearth, making an effort to thaw the air in my very cold house.

I shouldn't say I was surprised. Sam didn't knock. He opened the door and came in. "Well," I said, trying to emphasize the irritation in my voice, "just make yourself at home."

"Don't mind if I do," he answered, missing the point. "A might chilly in here," he said, going to the hearth and warming his hands.

"Damned freezing," I said. "You forgot the little matter about butane. Tank's empty, and I don't have a phone, or any way to get word to the delivery truck—know what I mean?"

He turned a serious eye on me, asked, "Your car broke-down?"

Shaking my head I said, "I'm from Los Angeles. Remember? It doesn't snow in Los Angeles. I don't know how to drive in this stuff."

"Not a thing to worry about. I'll phone an order in for you when I get back to my son's house. You got some coffee?"

I rolled my eyes and went to the kitchen, measured grounds and water, and plugged my automatic drip machine in. I'd almost forgotten my own craving for a cup of the stuff. While it brewed, I returned to the living room and took a seat opposite Sam on the right side of the hearth.

"You got a key for that workshop?" I asked.

"Sure, that's the one I gave you."

"What about a house key?"

"Same key."

One problem down, I thought. "Who owns the chickens?" I asked.

"Ben," he said. He paused, scratched his chin, added, "Ben likes animals. Found a horse last summer. Knew it belonged to somebody, had a bridle and saddle on. Let him keep it till one of them animal-control trucks drove up, asking a bunch of questions. Had to show 'em where it was. They hauled it off. Ben got awful shook up 'bout that. He thought their truck was some kinda kachina. Thought it would be real dis'pointed in him. Ben and his folks, well they think like that, you know. Things they can't explain always have something to do with their kachinas. These people'd be lost without them kachinas. They're the messengers, you know. Them kachinas. They bring messages and good luck, stuff like that, from the gods. The gods send 'em here, you know."

I was trying hard to follow what Sam was talking about. "Ben?" I asked, focusing on one thing at a time.

"Yeah. Ben's a youngster. 'Bout twelve, I reckon. One of your neighbors. Suspect you'll get along with Ben pretty good. Kopeki's a bird of a different century," he laughed, "Old buzzard will get right heavy on your nerves. Likes coffee, too. Real odd, him liking coffee. You wouldn't think those folks would drink..." Sam's voice cracked and he began to cough. He pulled a huge handkerchief from his jeans pocket, blew his nose.

"Is there wood in the workshop?" I asked, wondering if Sam was making all this up. Maybe he was senile. I stared at his creviced face, decided he must be eighty...at the least.

"Wood's in the woodpile."

"Where's the woodpile?"

"Behind the workshop."

"Someone brought this wood in while I was out walking this morning," I said with a tilt of my head to indicate the freshly filled wood bin. "You got any idea who would do that?"

"Probably Ben. Kopeki ain't worth a damn when it comes to helpin' out with chores. 'Course his wife's a good worker, but you'd keep clear of her if you was smart. Real snippy woman."

"What's her name?" I asked, testing to see if he had to think up a name.

"Nakani."

Deciding to test a bit further, I asked, "Is Ben their grandson?"

"Ben? No. Ben ain't even from their century. I reckon they're related, clans and that sort of thing. Come to think of it," he paused, scratched his chin, "maybe they ain't related. Kopeki's folks traveled up from another pueblo when he was just a little feller..." Sam's voice trailed off with his thoughts.

Their century? This Kopeki and his wife must be older than the fossil! They'd have to be in their nineties. While I considered this, Sam went out to the kitchen and poured two cups of coffee, brought them back to the hearth, handed me one.

"You dilute it?" he asked.

"Dilute what?"

"Your coffee. Some people dump sugar and milk into a perfectly good brew, ruin it all to hell."

I smiled, nodded, took a sip. The coals were burning down, so I reached into the bin, chose a thick log, placed it on the coals. By now I was thinking these people might exist. Might. Still, that didn't explain why they didn't leave footprints.

"Sam..."

"Yeah?" he looked up from his cup.

"These people, they're from the same clan, you say. What's that mean?"

"Why, you know. Families. Clans. Like, say, the Mole People Clan, or the Deer People Clan, or the Red Corn People Clan. But like I said, I ain't sure 'bout Kopeki..."

"Indian clans?" I interrupted.

"No," he said, grinning. "They don't think of themselves as Indians. That ain't their word, you know."

I nodded, understood where the word came from, remembered what I'd thought about the "Pueblo People" label.

He set his empty cup on the hearth and stared at a place in his memory. He said, "Yeah. I've known these people since I was a real young fellow. Fact is, I've know them most of my life. Why, when my son was born, near sixty years ago, Nakani took it on herself to be the one who looked for the right name for the kid. Anyway, she isolated herself away from the rest of us for 'bout a week. When she reappeared, she came to me and told me what his name was supposed to be."

Sam went to the kitchen, poured himself more coffee, returned. I waited, but he seemed to be finished with the story.

"So what's your sons name?" I asked, impatient.

Sam looked at me with surprise. "Sam," he said.

"Sam? This woman hides away for days, then reappears only to give your kid your name?"

"Thought it was real appropriate," Sam said. I shrugged and shook my head.

We both sat in silence for a while, until Sam thought of something and started up again. "Was this same fireplace," he said.

"What?"

"This is where I kept a fire burning for eight days. Nakani said it was necessary. She's damned bossy, that woman. Don't know how old Kopeki tolerated her all these years. Made me use flint and steel to start it up, she did. Made me watch it day and night. Kept it going, I did."

"Your wife didn't think this was crazy?"

"Come to think of it," Sam said, "I reckon she did. She got tired of them—the neighbors. Took little Sam to Santa Fe. She lived there till she passed on to her other place."

"Other place?" I figured he meant heaven or hell.

"Don't know," he said. "Where ever it was she went to when she died. Didn't come back here." He winked, "I didn't imagine she would, though, not liking the neighbors."

I suddenly felt sad for him. He was an ancient, senile widower who made up a bunch of strange people to keep himself company in his lonely life. "Snow isn't letting up," I said, pointing out the window. "You should get back to town before evening. The highway's going to be treacherous enough as it is."

Sam seemed to agree. He stood up, pulled on his coat, and was half-way out the door when he turned around. "Almost forgot why I came to see you," he said. "Christmas is coming up in a few weeks. I'll be driving up to get Kopeki and Ben, and some of the others. We always go down to San Felipe for the big ceremony. You're welcome to ride along, if you'd like."

"What kind of ceremony?" I asked, not wanting to be contaminated by some one else's religious ideas.

"San Felipe is the Christmas Pueblo," Sam said. "After the Midnight Mass there's a real special dance tribute. You don't have to be Catholic. We ain't, but Kopeki and some of the other old-timers like the socializing. Nakani won't go to the Christmas Pueblo 'cause she can't understand the ceremony. She ain't one to go into something just for the social part. Don't get me wrong. She likes most of the pueblo ceremonies. Goes with us every time to the Green Corn Dance over at Santo Domingo. That's in August. 'Course her favorite is the one we just went to. . .down there at the Zuni Pueblo. Now that's a long drive! You know where it's at? That Zuni Pueblo?"

I nodded. It was near Gallup, close to the Arizona border. I'd noticed it on my map when I drove into New Mexico.

Sam noted my nod and went on, "That's the ceremony for the Time of the Walking Gods. It's real spectac'lar, it is." He was scratching his chin again. "I'll bet you'd learn somethin' there, 'bout them kachinas. You'd best remind me next year so you can go with us. These kachinas are the real powerful ones. Shalako. They call 'em that. Got six of 'em. Ten feet tall, you know, them Shalakos." He was grinning. "'Course they're partic'lar gods, and them Zuni folks believe if them Shalako ever quit showing up, that'll be the end of the Zuni."

"How many of these ceremony things are there?" I asked, wondering if he was making all this up, too.

"Reckon we go coupla times a season. Here I am letting all the warm air outta the house. I'll give them butane people a call, have them bring you a delivery right away." With that he was off, crunching through deep snow.

I watched out the window while he drove off, wondering if there was such a thing as a Christmas Pueblo. Picking up the empty cups, I went to the kitchen, cleaned up the egg-mess on the floor, and heated a can of soup.

5

I tested my key, discovered Sam was right. It fit all the locks. He was also right about the wood; there was a lot of it stacked neatly in rows against the back of the workshop. A large army-green canvas tarp covered the wood, kept it free from snow, and dry.

The workshop was empty, except for two work tables. It had a clean concrete floor, almost too clean to have recently been used. I sized it up, saw plenty of room for clay projects, and perhaps a few plaster molds and a couple of gallons of slip to add variety.

The workshop wasn't adobe, like my house. It was a more modern frame and stucco structure. Luckily, it was also wired, and had a light fixture in the ceiling. I was fitting a new bulb into the fixture when I heard a large diesel making its way slowly down the snow packed driveway. I poked my head out the door, was excited to see a butane delivery truck. Hurrying, as best I could through two feet of frozen powder, I met the driver when he stopped, near the tank.

"Almost didn't make it up today," the driver said, crawling from the cab. "Snow plows having trouble keeping the highway clear."

"I've been waiting all week," I replied. "Sam Hoskins was supposed to phone an order in three days ago."

"Hoskins did call it in. Like I said, lady, we couldn't get the truck up here. Case you haven't noticed, this snow ain't melting. Look, I got two more stops after you, so how much you want?"

"I want the tank filled."

"You paying with a credit card? Can't take a check."

"Cash."

"You keep that kinda money around?" He raised his eyebrows, eyed me with suspicion.

"Why should you care how I pay, long as the money's good?" I asked, adding, "I don't believe in credit cards."

He shrugged and crawled up into the cab, pulled the truck alongside the tank, rearranged hoses and pushed buttons, then walked over to where I stood while the tank filled. "Old man who lived here was a real nut-case," he said casually.

"You know Sam?"

"Delivered his butane for near ten years, now. Guess the place got to be too much work for him. Surprised hell out of me when he said he was selling out. Seemed 'bout as attached to the land as a cow is to its calf."

I stared at him, wondering why he thought Sam was a nut-case. Probably same reason I thought so. "You ever make deliveries to my neighbors?" I asked.

Removing his Stetson, he ran a gloved hand over his bushy brown hair and shook his head. "Lady, you ain't got no neighbors."

"What about . . ."

The man placed his hat back on his head and interrupted my inquiry. "Tank's full." With that, he crossed to the tank, unfastened hoses, and handed me a bill.

"I'll get your money," I said, hurrying into the house. I pulled a flour tin down from the cabinet over my stove, took out a handful of assorted bills, was ready to count them when I saw the eggs. A dozen or more in a most unusual basket with feathers woven densely into the fiber coils. They were carefully positioned with pointed ends up, a trick to preserve freshness. I touched one; it was warm. Quite a trick, I thought, since it was freezing outside. Unless these were just deposited, or laid, or whatever it was chickens did when they made eggs.

I finished counting the money and started out the back door, hesitated, went to the kitchen for the basket of eggs, took both to the delivery man. Offering the money, I assured him, "It's correct down to the dollar."

He counted it anyway, and tried not to notice the basket of eggs. Finally he asked, "Those for me?"

"No," I said. "Just wanted to know if you could see them."

He wrinkled his brow and got into his truck and left.

This confirmed it. The eggs were real beyond my seeing them, eating them, smashing them on the floor; even beyond Sam's telling me they were real.

When my morning chores were completed, I donned two pairs of my warmest socks and my only boots, filled a plastic bucket with hot water, and set out to visit Ben's chickens. While I walked my eyes searched the snow for tracks. Coyote prints and tracks belonging to what could have been a large bobcat or a small cougar crossed my property. Nothing else. No signs of Ben, who I was sure brought the eggs.

To my surprise the courtyard at the pueblo was empty. Suddenly I thought about the predators whose tracks I'd just seen. Of course! The cougar, or maybe the coyotes, came and ate Rooster and his Happy Hens. It would be easy for animals such as these to sneak in through the underground tunnel. No. Why would they even have to sneak, when they could attack from this courtyard. I whistled through my teeth and slapped my thigh in disgust and self-castigation for not thinking about the chickens' safety earlier. Might as well empty the bucket in the snow and go home, I decided. But Rooster craned his cocky little head out the doorway to see who owned the whistle before I dumped the water.

"What's this?" I whispered. His head popped back into the pueblo, so I hurried in after him, saw him fly through the horse room and land on a pile of crumbled adobe and rock in one corner. A soft clucking began when I entered the room, and as I glanced around, it was obvious all the chickens were here. I poured the water into the tin pan, tried to remember if this was where I'd left the pan, was almost sure it wasn't. Didn't matter. I needed to figure out a way to prevent the obvious abundance of predators from killing Ben's chickens.

A voice distracted me. I strained my ears to hear it again. Silence. Then. There—a man's voice, an old voice, talking to . . . himself I imagined, in a strange tongue. Not Spanish, or anything else I could identify. He was somewhere in this pueblo, towards the corn room—at least that's how I thought of the room with the shelves and fire hole. I don't know why, it simply looked like a corn room; not that I knew what a corn room looked like.

This time the black hole, or corridor, seemed larger, stretching out farther than I remembered; maybe because I purposely tried to be quiet, taking short steps, placing my boot soles softly on the debris-strewn ground.

His words grew louder as I walked, until I knew he was in the corn room. With a stalking grace that surprised me, I crawled through the cracks and wall openings without making a sound. And there he was.

If Sam was a fossil, this man was a prehistoric relic! He sat— the temperature below freezing—practically naked on a colorful woven cloth. His feet were tucked beneath him, his hair was white as new crop cotton, and his skin was baked a crusty brown by lengthy exposure to sunlight. Surrounding him were half a dozen pottery bowls filled with different colors of corn kernels. At least another half dozen baskets, filled with what looked like beans, grains, assorted seeds, and pinon nuts, were mixed among the bowls of corn. I didn't need to strain my eyes to see. It was odd, but the room was well lighted, and for the first time I noticed the walls were coated with a type of whitewash. The man held something large, a leather mask. He began to fill his mouth with the contents of each container, chewing corn, beans, grain, seeds, and nuts. After he did this for a few minutes, he spit the resulting concoction onto the mask and rubbed it vigorously into the leather. All the while he was saying, "Si Kesi tom ho' ho'i yakapa. Hom to' tatcilikan a. Tom ho' toconanaka ho'i yakapa. To'yam tse-'makwin tsume ho'na yani ktciana. Holo awan tewan yo'apa to' kacima ceman tekana. Si len a kya tom ho' ho'i yakaka."

Now he faced the east wall and held the mask first to the east, then to the north, then to the west, next to the south, then to the sky, and finally to the center. He said, "Temla tekwi u'lohna' il-apona ton lukia yatena tsume." With this done he picked up what appeared to be white clay, calling the clay "hekohakwa." He rubbed the hekohakwa into the mask, and placed the mask in a bright sunny corner of the corn room.

I held my silence, not wanting to give myself away, and especially not wanting to be caught spying on what was probably a sacred ceremony. I waited. More than an hour passed before the old man resumed his work on the mask. This time he used a large piece of rabbit fur, dipped it into a stone container, and drew it out saturated with a blue dye. I heard him say "hecamu'le," as if introducing the blue stuff to the mask. Now he said, "Si hom he-kia tehya tom cinanaka ho' yam tca'le yakapa," while painting the mask blue.

When all seemed complete, he carried the mask to another room in the pueblo, and returned without it. I was considering sneaking off before he could notice me when I heard a young child's voice. I glanced round, realized the child was in the corn room speaking to the old man. The child handed the man a fistful of feathers, then sat on his small heels and waited, as if for a story. And sure enough, the old man told the child a very long story. I couldn't understand their tongue, and decided this was a good time to steal off.

I was backing away from the crumbled doorway behind which I'd kept myself hidden, when I bumped into another old man.

"Whoa!" I said loudly, and with extreme surprise.

"Ah," he said, "I see you also are watching my memory."

"Wha...?"

"You are understanding this?" he asked, ignoring my shock. I shook my head no.

"Ah," he said again. "Well, it is a very sacred thing. Not for woman to see, so it cannot matter if you don't understand."

My curiosity was now at a peak, and I managed to say, "Since I've already watched, why don't you tell me what it's about."

His eyes were amused, and he seemed to be deciding something, when suddenly he reached into a pocket of his trousers and removed a roll of corn husk, tossed it to the ground near my boots. I stooped and picked it up, saw that it was a crude sort of cigarette: tobacco leaves wrapped in corn husk.

"So you accept my offering," he said.

I shrugged.

"We will sit and smoke," he said.

"I never smoke."

He ignored me and sat on the cold ground. I sat down with him. He lit the crude cigarette using a very antique fire-drill, revolving it from right to left until it sparked. He took a drag on the cigarette and gave it to me. I did the same thing. Then he grinned broadly and said, "It is done. We can never be enemies now that the offer is accepted. It is unbreakable."

I shook my head, thinking he was a bit dramatic, and wondered for the first time who he was, and what he meant about my watching his memory. He seemed to be reading my mind, and replied, "I am Kopeki. Are you a ho'i?"

"A what?"

"A live person. Are you?"

"Yes. What else would I be?"

"Maybe you are a witch, or a kachina."

"I've heard about you," I changed the subject. "My name is Dana Whitehawk. I bought Sam Hoskin's place. I'm living there now."

"White-hawk," he said, separating the words. "Are you a hawk who becomes a person?"

"No."

"Are you a person who becomes a hawk?"

"No. I'm pretty much myself all the time."

He grinned, asked, "If you are not a witch, and you are not a kachina, how are you able to see my memories?"

"I don't know what you mean," I said. "I was watching the old fellow making some kind of a mask. When he finished with his work, I saw the child take him a handful of feathers."

"Yes," Kopeki nodded. "It was something I was thinking about, a time when I was a small boy."

"You're telling me that—the entire scenario—was nothing more than a memory?"

"Memory is very much more than most things," Kopeki said. "I am, you see, a memory of myself."

"If you say so," I said, thinking Kopeki was more senile than Sam.

"White-hawk," Kopeki was saying, repeating my last name quietly to himself, deciding about me. He stood up and began walking out of the room, into the corridor. I followed him to the horse room. He sat in the straw. Rooster went to him and he stroked the chicken's silky feathers with one hand while he rubbed his bare chin with the other. I sat in the straw opposite and watched. Kopeki had the same crusty brown skin and cottony white hair that the relic in the corn room had. But Kopeki was dressed in baggy pants, a loose-fitting jersey, and he wore a baseball cap. Quite ordinary, but inappropriate in snow.

Finally he looked up and said, "You are the medicine of the white hawk. That is good. Well, I am the memory of Kopeki, and I enjoy coming and going between the sacred mountains and visiting the village of my people's memories."

"That's great," I said.

"I especially enjoy watching television with my friend, Sam."

"Right," I said.

"Sam's kachina took him away," Kopeki continued. "Haven't enjoyed watching television since Sam is away."

"Sam moved to Santa Fe," I said, wondering why Kopeki thought a kachina took Sam away. Then I remembered Sam said Ben thought the animal control truck was a kachina. I added, "Sam's staying with his son."

"Do you enjoy television?" Kopeki asked, not listening to my explanations about Sam.

"Some," I said, "Why?"

"I'll come watch television with you."

I started to object, thought about the ritual in the corn room, decided to make a deal.

6

Kopeki thought about my proposition for a few minutes, and the television kachina won out. He agreed to tell me "a few safe and less important" details about the mask making ritual, and he promised to share with me the story the old man told him.

"He wasn't telling you the story," I corrected, "He was telling the child."

"The child was me, the man was the Otakamosi, a kiva chief," Kopeki said. He seemed to believe that, so I let it be. "We were still in the place I was born, before we came here. It was my memory," he reminded. "I can put a memory anywhere. I put it here."

"Explain," I said. "Begin with the seed chewing part."

"The seeds bring life to what you call the mask. It helps when we need strength and rain. Then the mask must be presented properly to each of the six sacred directions. Now the mask is made smooth using hekohakwa. When this is dry, the mask is made forever sacred with hecamu'le."

Kopeki sat there, a happy little grin on his face, thinking this information would satisfy me.

"More," I said.

He raised his eyebrows.

"You want to watch my television, finish talking."

"What is it you still don't know?"

"What was the kiva chief telling the boy...you?"

"You would understand all of these things," Kopeki said, his look turning sly while he eyed me suspiciously.

It was my turn to raise my eyebrows.

"Where do you come from, kachina-magician-who-calls-self-white-hawk? Ho' ceman. Tom tewan tse'makwin."

"Say what?"

"I call you, day spirit. What trick do you play? Only a kachina magician can watch the memory of a man who was once ho'i, but who has not been so since the times when the enemies came riding horses."

"Good grief! All I want to know is what that old kiva chief was saying. I'm not a magician. I don't even know any card tricks, okay? I'm leaving," I said, getting up and starting out of the pueblo.

Kopeki was right behind me, saying, "You have already smoked the sacred smoke. You are bound to be at peace with me forever. This cannot be broken..."

I turned around and said, "I'm not your enemy, I'm your neighbor, but you're a bit eccentric and you don't keep your word very well, so I'm going home. It's freezing cold."

"I keep my word!"

"You haven't told me what the chief was saying. I didn't understand the language he was speaking, and I don't understand you when you start blabbering in...whatever it is you're speaking."

"Ah," he said, "You are testing me. You are wise, White-Hawk." From his tone I could tell he was revising my last name and making it my only name. Fine. I could live with that.

He added, "I will travel to your home, and tell you what this Otakamosi from my memory was saying. Then you will let me watch television."

I shrugged and we both started to climb the steps, make our way through the snow to my house. He walked behind me. I forgot to check to see if he left footprints in the snow.

The first thing Kopeki said upon entering the door into my dining room was, "It is a good day for coffee."

I was busy wondering how he stayed warm, wearing only trousers, a jersey sweater, leather slippers without socks, and that ridiculous baseball hat.

Kopeki cleared his throat and repeated, "It is a good day for coffee."

"You and Sam not too shy about drinking up my brew," I said through clenched teeth, more to myself than him. I draped my coat over a dining room chair, pulled my boots and socks off and left them under the chair, and went into my kitchen, put a full pot on to brew. I found Kopeki kneeling on the hearth before my fireplace, blowing at a few dying coals. He'd placed a large pine log on top of the coals.

"Thanks," I said, sitting in one of the chairs close to the hearth. Kopeki glanced around the living room, went to the sofa, removed a knit blanket, then spread it on the floor before the hearth and sat on the blanket. For some reason I thought about the chickens and all the predators. "Kopeki," I said, "Does Ben put the chickens somewhere safe at night?"

"I think they are not in danger."

"They could be. I saw coyote and large cat tracks near the pueblo this morning."

"Oh," he laughed. "You're looking at animals making tracks. There is no danger from these."

I thought about that for a few moments, decided if he didn't care about the chickens, I didn't care either. "Okay, fine. Now, about . . ."

He raised his nose into the air, inhaled, said, "Ah, the water has become coffee."

Eventually he was settled on the blanket, full cup of coffee in hand. I waited. Finally the story was told.

"A good memory comes from when I was a small boy," Kopeki began. "The Otakamosi—these are all words you understand, but they are not the correct words—anyway, the Otakamosi was preparing a kachina mask. This I have told you about. After the mask was ready for feathers, he asked me to bring him eagle feathers. It took me a long time to find eagle feathers. When I put them in his hand, I asked the Otakamosi, 'Why do you use eagle feathers? There are so many more turkey feathers.'

"'Sit, be patient, and listen,' he told me."

"Once a young boy who was the son of a kachina chief was dropped high on a mountain by a witch. On this mountain there was a witch boy, and he often played games with the lost boy. One time witch boy grabbed a black ant and rubbed lost boy's flesh with the ant. Witch boy then told lost boy, 'The ant will keep you safe from all harm.'

"Another time, witch boy plucked a hoop from the sky and jumped through it, turning into a chipmunk. He instructed lost boy to do the same, and lost boy turned into a chipmunk, also.

Together they ran through the mountain searching for bird's eggs. When witch boy was tired of the game, he jumped back through the hoop and became himself. Lost boy followed, also becoming himself again. Witch boy then ran away, leaving lost boy without food or water for four days.

"Lost boy cried until an eagle who had a nest nearby heard. Eagle flew into the sky, circling among the clouds four times, until his keen eyes spotted lost boy sitting on the mountain. Eagle set himself down next to lost boy, but the boy continued to cry. Eagle removed his dress of feathers, and lost boy looked up, saw a man. 'I am thirsty and hungry,' lost boy said, 'and I want to go home.' The man said, 'Crawl on my back. I will carry you home.' Lost boy tried, but was too weak. The man put his dress of feathers back on and became an eagle.

"Lost boy clasped his weak arms around the eagle's neck, and the eagle carried him back to his village. Eagle plucked feathers from his tail, and down from beneath his wings, and gave these to the boy, who was no longer lost. 'Do not allow anyone but your father, who is a kachina chief, to touch these feathers,' the eagle said. 'Your father will know what to do with them.'

"After eagle flew back up to the mountain, a woman from the village saw the boy with the feathers. She ran and touched them, and turned into an owl, then flew away to live forever beside the spring. The boy hurried home. His father was happy to see him, and wanted to know how he survived while he was lost. 'It was because of the eagle,' the boy said. 'Eagle gave these feathers to me after he brought me home, and he said I must give them only to you, a kachina chief. Eagle said you would know what to do with them. A woman who touched them is now an owl living beside the spring. Are these feathers magic?'

"The father took the feathers and said, 'Eagles have magic that is good and strong and wise, and I know what to do with these feathers. I must use them when making the kachina mask. From now on, kachina masks will always have eagle feathers, unless there is a very good reason for them not to.'

"And that is why kachinas always have eagle feathers."

Kopeki leaned back on his heels and said, "It is a very good day for another cup of coffee."

"Is that it?" I asked.

"That is what the Otakamosi was saying to me. That is my memory."

I took Kopeki's cup and refilled it. I found him still sitting on the blanket, but he'd moved in front of the television. I handed him the remote control, said, "Watch whatever makes you happy."

He stared at the control, confused. I took it back, showed him how to select channels by pressing the square buttons. As I was leaving the living room to attend to my housework chores, I heard the channels popping back and forth. And I heard Kopeki laughing joyously.

7

Kopeki had spent the previous morning, and the greater part of the afternoon, clicking the remote control, whizzing from one program to the next, and enjoying himself to capacity. I cleaned and lined cupboards and closets, scoured the bathroom, filled my wood bin with kindling and logs, and was reminded of Sam's words: "Kopeki ain't worth a damn when it comes to helpin' out with chores."

"Got that one right," I said to myself. It was now mid-morning the following day. I sat in my dining room staring out the window, wondering about the people Sam described. Kopeki was everything Sam had said. Well, almost everything. He wasn't really that old. Hard to tell, but I guessed he was somewhere between sixty or seventy. Certainly younger than Sam by a decade or two.

I hated to admit it, but I wasn't minding having neighbors as much as I tried to think I was. Still, one question was not answered, "Where did they actually live?" The pueblo hadn't been lived in for—I guessed because of its present state—about one, maybe one and a half centuries. And there was the big curiosity about what Kopeki called his "memory." However, I'd never been one to worry unduly about things I couldn't immediately explain. Such mysteries always made me think of something one of my teachers said when I was a child: "Every problem has its solution."

That'd been good enough for me then, and it was good enough now. My neighbors lived nearby. Ben had some chickens and once kidnapped a horse belonging to someone else. Kopeki liked coffee and television, and Kopeki's wife was supposedly a pain to have around. I imagined the snow would be melting soon, since it was a mild day and already the sun was bright overhead. When the snow melted I could explore the land beyond the pueblo cliff, and perhaps see their house.

Early that afternoon, while filling the bucket with warm water for the chickens, I heard the door into my living room open and close. I'm going to have to teach them to knock, I thought, and then I felt a hard object slam across my shoulder. The impact threw me to my knees, and I tried to roll sideways, keep the next blow away from my head.

"Where's your money, bitch!" a male voice yelled. A strong hand gripped my arm like a vice, pulled me to my feet, swung me around.

He was heavy-set, in his late twenties or early thirties, and his black hair was slicked tight against his crown. My first instinct was to shrink away, and I could feel a sensation engulfing me: Panic! It unfurled itself, paralyzed my lungs, tried to suffocate me with weakness. Despised weakness! Already it was diffusing easily, setting its course to saturate my system. My heart was pumping too fast; my free hand went quickly to my chest, tried to hide the rapid pounding. Too late. My hand was trembling out of control, my body betrayed me with its feeble shaking. Be brave! I commanded myself. My Judas ears turned traitor, pretended not to hear.

But fear has strength. I jerked the arm he held free from his crushing grasp and fled through the dining room, had my hand on the back door knob, was trying to get it open. His noisy footsteps pursued and his speed overpowered me. I felt like an insect trapped beneath its predator's shadow. Then his angry heavy breathing brushed my vulnerable neck, and he hit me across the back. This time with his fist. The pain sent electric shocks shooting throughout my body. He swung me around and was folding his hand into a tight fist, aiming for my face, when the egg hit him.

For a moment his ferocious temper turned into surprise, and he raised his hand to finger the sticky mess which clung to his hair and stuck to his scalp. Slowly he looked behind to see where it came from, and another egg smashed into the side of his cheek.

While he was distracted I reached backwards, pushed the door open, got outside and raced for my workshop. Once inside I bolted the door and shoved one of the tables in front of it. Seconds passed before I heard the man again. This time he was shouting in Spanish, but not at me. I recognized a few of the words, especially the ones meaning witch, sorcery, witchcraft. I chanced a quick look out the small window, saw him stumbling backwards through the mud and snow, moving away from my house. All the while eggs kept flying through the air, breaking across his face and chest. I couldn't see anyone else. Just airborne eggs and the intruder.

My heart continued to race at a rate that made me dizzy. I was afraid he would break the workshop door, beat me to death with those huge horrible fists. I was cornered. I would have to fight for my life. My fingers seemed to turn into claws, and I could almost believe I was sharpening them. I imagined myself striking his cheek with razor sharp talons, tearing off his flesh, making him shrink away to experience pain as intense as what he'd caused me. I slipped to the ground and huddled under the other table, waiting.

Nothing happened.

Then I heard a light rapping on the door.

"White-Hawk woman?"

At first I hesitated. Again the voice spoke, "White-Hawk woman?" It was the voice of a young boy.

"Ben?" I whispered through the door.

"Hello," he replied. "I am Ben. Are you White-Hawk woman?"

I pulled the table away and slowly opened the door, saw a slender boy of average height with a smooth ivory complexion and blue-black hair which hung past his shoulders. He was wearing faded slacks, a long sleeve heavy shirt, and holding what was left of a basket of eggs. I stepped out and looked at the three eggs in the large basket. Hardly what I would call lethal weapons.

"How'd you chase that man away?" I asked.

He ignored my question, held out the eggs, said, "I brought this food offering for you."

"Thank you," I said, still shaking, worried the man would return. I glanced all around.

"He is gone," Ben said, noting my fear. "He will probably die today, or maybe tomorrow. Did you see the pahos I put out for you? I hope there were enough. I made them myself."

My confusion must've been obvious.

"This is the killing ground," Ben explained, gesturing to include all my property. "The man-who-is-enemy offended you, White-Hawk woman-who-protects-the-killing-ground. He will die."

"Let's get back into the house," I said, still trying to see where the intruder had gone. I added, "After we lock the doors, you can tell me what you're talking about."

Ben was more familiar with my house and its contents than I. He took milk from the refrigerator, added cocoa, poured it into a pan and heated it. I sat in my dining room and allowed him to serve me a large mug of hot chocolate. I'd have preferred coffee, but I watched as he poured himself a mug and sipped it slowly, savoring the taste. He made it look so good. I took a sip, and then another, until I began to feel almost calm.

I didn't talk, and he took my cue. We sat in silence until our cocoa was finished, then we went to the living room. I think I'd half expected him to behave like Kopeki, choosing a blanket on the floor instead of a comfortable chair. Not Ben. He immediately picked the best chair before the hearth. I sat in the remaining chair, and we both watched the yellows, oranges and blues in the fire's small flame.

Fear was first in my thoughts and I tried to will my hands to stop trembling. That such a barbarous man would leave after being pelted with fragile eggs—well, it was impossible to believe. I glanced at the young boy seated across from me, could see he had none of the same thoughts. The man was simply my enemy, the way Ben perceived it, and not only would he not be back, but he would die for having offended me.

"Ben," I began, choosing my words carefully. "Ben, I wonder if you could tell me why you said I was...what did you call me? Protector of the killing ground? Am I living on some kind of battleground...maybe a graveyard? And what is a pahos?" The idea didn't alarm me. Dead bodies were empty things, what was left of a person's physical machine when it wore out. I always imagined a person was much more than a physical machine.

"Pahos," Ben said, watching me suspiciously, "are what Sam calls prayer sticks. Also, the burial place is there." He extended his arm, pointed in the direction which was beyond the pueblo, toward the foot hills of the upper canyon. "This is the killing ground," he said, thinking I understood.

"What is a killing ground?"

Ben's smile grew until his white teeth showed. "Kopeki told me about you. He said you were a wise trickster magician and enjoyed asking questions to see how we answered. You must be a very powerful White-Hawk magician. I hope my simple offerings will please you so you will stay and protect our killing ground. Sam protected our killing ground until he went away."

I had to approach this a different way. Already I was thinking less about my earlier intruder, was getting drawn into wanting to understand this new thing. I said, "I apologize for not thanking you for the prayer sticks...pahos." In my mind I could see them, stuck in the ground on either side of my driveway: short sticks with chicken feathers tied to the tops. I'd almost forgotten them, having only noticed them the evening I'd arrived. I hadn't thought about who put them there, or why. Seemed natural, to see prayer sticks in this part of New Mexico. Now I realized Ben put them there for me, thinking I was here to guard over something. I wondered if pahos was his word for prayer sticks, or a Spanish word. I'd never heard it before.

While I mused over these small details surrounding my new home, a noise like two box-cars crashing together pierced the silence of the countryside. I jumped to my feet and started for the door. Outside I strained to listen, but heard no other sound. I donned my jacket and boots, and prepared to go in search of the cause of the commotion. Ben sat in his chair watching, making no effort to join me. "You coming?" I asked. I wanted to discover what'd happened, but I didn't want to go alone. I hadn't entirely forgotten about the man.

Behaving quite like a boy of twelve, he shrugged and grumbled and came with me—in protest.

We walked at a quick pace down my now mud-slushy driveway, past my fence, and were almost to the end of the county road, where it turned sharply to meet the highway, when we spotted the car. It was a burgundy Monte Carlo. The nose of the Monte Carlo was smashed into the ditch and the tail lights protruded into the air. The back tires were spinning free since they weren't touching the ground. I started to run towards the wreck. This time Ben followed on my heels.

Upon reaching the car I noticed deep gouges in the slush and snow where the driver of the car had tried to negotiate the turn while going too fast. Instead the car had plunged straight ahead, crashing into the ditch's immovable bank. I hesitated to look inside, but Ben was already there.

"Your enemy is dead," Ben said.

"You sure?" I asked, lowering myself into the ditch, peering in through the broken glass. I couldn't see his face, but from the back of the head I was sure. It was the man who attacked me. My enemy.

Ben was being careful not to touch the car. He looked up at me, said, "This is a powerful kachina. I think we should leave."

"I think I should try to flag a car down out on the highway," I said. "I don't want him sitting out here, rotting, so close to my house. Maybe I should call the sheriff. Is there a telephone at your house?"

Ben shook his head no, climbed out of the ditch, started to leave.

"Wait a minute," I called, joining him on the county road. "I've changed my mind. I'm going back for my car. There's got to be a house up the highway. Hopefully someone'll have a telephone so I can phone the sheriff."

Ben said nothing.

"I need you to go with me," I said. "At least until I reach the highway...in case I get stuck in this mud. I'll need you to push the car, or steer while I push. Okay?"

He shrugged, and I accepted that as agreement.

To my surprise, the Honda kept its tracking, and we made it safely to the highway. When I stopped, Ben climbed out. "Ben," I called. He turned around. "I'm indebted to you," I said. "You come over anytime you want." He smiled, nodded and left.

8

Snowplows and regular traffic kept the asphalt highway free from most of the ice and slush which covered the dirt road leading to my house. I hesitated before turning onto the highway, tried to recall the last house I'd seen before arriving at my own turnoff. I couldn't remember seeing any kind of structure for quite a few miles. Then I thought about what the butane delivery man had said. He'd said he had two more deliveries to make up the road. Up the road could be less than one mile. Or it could be ten miles. One way to find out. I shifted into first and set out to find a house with a phone.

I'd traveled less than three miles when I spotted a mobile home. It was a white oblong box-shaped structure with a flat roof. Two cars were parked near the front doorsteps. I slowed to almost a crawl and searched the side of the highway for a driveway entrance. I found it a few hundred feet up the road.

This was a much better driveway than mine: hard-packed gravel. As I pulled the Honda to a stop beside one of the cars, the mobile home's front door opened and a short, obese gray-haired woman stepped out. A black shawl was draped across her shoulders.

"Hello," I said, getting out of my car. "My name is Dana Whitehawk." I gestured in the direction I'd come and added, "I bought the old place down the road. . .where Sam Hoskins used to live."

"Sí," she said, her skeptical expression changed quickly into a broad smile. "Sam Hoskins. Sí, sí. Buenos días, señora? Señorita? Me llamo María."

I knew she was telling me her name was María, and she was greeting me politely, wondering if I were married or an old maid. But my Spanish would never keep up with hers, so I simply shrugged and asked, "Habla usted inglés?"

"Oh, sí. Yes. I speak English."

"Bueno," I said. "Dígalo en inglés, por favor."

"Of course," she said apologetically, "I can speak English."

"Gracias. I'm sorry to bother you on such a nice day," I said, "but I don't have a telephone, and I was hoping you did. You see, someone had an accident, an automobile accident, near my house. I believe he is dead." I left out the part about nearly being beaten to death by the victim of this accident. I tried not to sound pleased that he was dead.

"Oh, my," she gasped, putting her hand to her mouth. "This is awful. I'm sorry. Please come inside." She stepped back into her house and made room for me to enter. "Have a seat. Aquí," she gestured to a chair and sofa. "I'll get you some coffee, then I'll ring up our policía."

I sat on the small sofa which was covered in brightly crocheted afghan quilts. Her mobile home was small and poorly furnished, but it was spotlessly clean. She brought me coffee, already ruined with cream and sugar. I thanked her and tried to sip it without making a face.

Her telephone hung on the wall between her kitchen and the small living room where I sat. She dialed a number and waited a few seconds, then began speaking rapidly in Spanish to the person on the other end. While she was talking, a short obese man who appeared to be older than María, emerged from the hallway. Dressed in baggy trousers and a white T-shirt, he yawned and rubbed his eyes, looked at me without much curiosity, and exited back down the hall. "Mi esposo," she whispered, forgetting to say "My husband" in English. A few minutes later she finished her conversation.

While we waited, she asked about Sam. I told her where he'd moved, told her he'd already been out to see me. For some reason, I didn't tell her about my neighbors.

Thirty minutes passed before I saw the sheriff's car pull into the driveway, parking next to my Honda. He got out, walked around to check out my license, then came to the door.

"You from California?" he asked me, soon as María invited him in.

I nodded.

"Need to get a New Mexico registration for that car if you're living here," he said. I nodded again. He rested his hand on his holster and turned his attention to María. "Cómo se llama?" he asked her, wanting to know what my name was.

"Dana Whitehawk," María said.

He turned back to me, asked, "Dónde vive usted?"

I was about to answer, tell him where I lived, when María told him, "Ella no habla español." Translated, she told him I didn't speak Spanish. I tried not to let them know I understood it quite well, as long as they spoke slowly.

He seemed pleased I couldn't eavesdrop, and quickly asked her, "La conoce usted?" María said no, that she didn't know me before that day. She asked him to sit down, and offered him refreshment, but he declined. Instead he stood by her door, twirling his uniform hat, and asked if I was as loco as Sam, and if I knew the old pueblo near my land had curses and spells, and all imaginable kinds of sorcery and witchcraft surrounding its history.

"Pooh," María replied, "Es imposible. Es una mujer bonita. No está loca. Estás equivocado."

María was on my side. She told him I was a pretty lady, that I wasn't crazy, that his assumptions were wrong.

He wasn't convinced. This time he said some things I found educational. He said he doubted I would have bought my house if I'd known it was built on the land where ancient Indians killed all the possessions of their dead. María interrupted, reminded him it was a long time ago. She said too many people had already been sifting my dirt for over a hundred years, that whatever items had been killed through the years there were long gone. I could tell María was not a superstitious woman, but I was pleased the sheriff was. Now I understood the meaning of Ben's 'killing-ground.' My land was where a dead person's properties, whether pottery, tools, weapons, clothes, or even animals, were destroyed when the person died. The idea was to send all a person's things with him to better insure his journey into the afterworld. I don't know why this didn't occur to me earlier, but I doubted these places were referred to as killing-grounds in any of the books I'd read.

I was busy assimilating this new knowledge when I heard the sheriff identify the dead man. He said the deceased's name was Luján—I didn't know if that was his first or last name—and he lived somewhere even further up the highway. He wasn't very well liked. Was a bit of a "pachuco," according to María. I gathered, from the sheriff's tone, Luján wasn't going to be missed by the 'policía,' either.

Suddenly the sheriff turned to me and asked, "What was Luján doing at your house?"

I explained to him, as carefully and calmly as I could manage. But I didn't mention Ben. Again, I don't know why. Maybe I didn't want to involve him or his family.

"How'd he know you kept cash in your house?" the sheriff asked.

I shrugged. Then I remembered the butane delivery driver. "I paid for my butane in large bills," I said. "The only person who knew about my cash was that driver."

The sheriff glanced at María. María said, "That truck brings butane here, then he goes up and makes another stop, probably Luján's brother's house. Maybe he said something to somebody there about her money. Not very smart. You can't trust any of Luján's relatives."

The sheriff seemed reluctantly satisfied with this theory. He started to leave, then he turned and asked, "Why was Luján covered with broken eggs?"

"I threw them at him," I lied.

"He quit beating you up and left without your money because you threw eggs at him?"

"I guess," I said.

The sheriff narrowed his suspicious eyes into slits, letting me know he didn't believe me. But I knew he would have to accept what I said because I wasn't a suspect, and Luján wasn't murdered; he killed himself trying to drive his car too fast on a road that was dangerously muddy.

Later, while driving home, I considered why I hadn't mentioned Ben, or any of my neighbors. The sheriff's ideas about the pueblo being haunted with curses amused me, and for some odd reason, I began to imagine a parade of masked kachinas dancing through the crumbling ruins.

At that instant a huge bird flew out of the sky, passed within inches of the Honda's windshield, and then it was gone. I don't know why, but all the kachinas that had been dancing in my thoughts suddenly turned into chickens.

9

My adventure with Luján, not more than two days behind me, seemed an eternity ago. By the time I'd returned from María's house, the Monte Carlo was being towed from the ditch, and the body had been removed. Taken to some funeral home, I guessed. I didn't actually care what they did with Luján, as long as he didn't rot near my property.

There'd been two men operating the tow truck, and a sheriff's car was parked opposite the truck. I didn't stop, and none of the men made any effort to get me to stop. No one came to my house later, either. I was happy to be done with the whole event.

The Christmas holiday arrived. I would have forgotten about Christmas if it hadn't been for the abundance of decorations covering every square foot of Santa Fe. Pushing, crushing, crowds of shoppers filled sidewalks, stores, and malls. I had to tolerate delays in long lines anywhere I went, and I found it necessary to get aggressive when I needed clerical help while buying supplies to improve my house.

My first purchase had been paint for the interior, and dozens of yards of fabric to make drapes for my bare windows. I'd already ripped out the horrible blue carpet, discovered good linoleum covering the floors, and decided I would rather have that than new wall-to-wall carpet. But I did want a few floor rugs. My last planned stop for the morning was at a discount warehouse department store. I selected a braided rug large enough to cover most of my bedroom, and a machine made pseudo-Navajo rug large enough to cover most of my living room. I'd have preferred a genuine Navajo rug, but I didn't have twenty thousand dollars. They were very expensive.

"You wanna bring your truck around to the delivery door?"

the young salesman in the rug department asked.

"What?"

"You got a truck for these rugs?" he asked. "They won't fit into a car; won't even fit a large station wagon. Lady, you need a truck."

Feeling naive and ridiculous for not having considered this small detail, I pretended I had everything in control. Then I remembered Sam's truck. It was full-size, and would easily haul the rugs. "A friend will pick them up for me," I said.

"We don't have, like, lay-away service, lady. Know what I mean?"

"My friend can pick them up today."

"They'll be at the delivery door," he said. "Just have your receipt ready."

I left the store mad. At myself. What if Sam didn't want to haul my rugs home? My stomach growled, let me know it was now past lunch time. I crawled into the Honda and started it up, sat in the parking lot a few minutes, trying to decide if I should call Sam, or come up with an alternative. A fast food hamburger chain across the street caught my attention, so I shut the engine off, walked over, and bought some lunch. While I was eating I noticed a newspaper laying on the seat of the chair next to me. I picked it up and began reading. On one of the pages an advertisement jumped out: Rent a truck by the hour. Reasonable rates.

Sure! I could rent a truck, haul the rugs to my house, have it back to Santa Fe in less than two hours. It was a great idea. I carried my cup to the counter, asked one of the youngsters behind the counter if I could have a refill on coffee. "Refills cost forty cents," she snapped. I dug change out of my handbag, gave her two quarters.

"Keep the change," I said, feeling suddenly generous and kind.

"We don't accept tips," the girl said with a glare that bordered on rude.

I accepted the dime and carried my coffee to the table, decided rudeness wasn't confined to California. At my table I found someone had removed the newspaper. Didn't matter. I could still see the advertisement in my mind, and the address listed a street nearby. It was the same street that accommodated the Turquoise Teepee.

A short time later, with help from one of the store employees, I was loading my rugs into a full size white Ford pickup. I'd already transferred the paints and fabrics into the truck, and was trying to think of anything else I might need that would require the Ford's services. A bed! How could I forget? Guess I'd gotten used to sleeping on the living room floor in my sleeping bag. I recalled seeing a mattress store near where I had lunch. I drove there, purchased the best set I could afford, and set off in the direction of home.

I could say I was surprised, but I wasn't. Ben was there. He'd dragged my wood bin into the front yard. The bin was tilted on its side and he was using a hand held whisk broom to sweep out every last splinter. Stacked neatly on the front steps was a pile of assorted pieces of wood: large logs, medium logs, chunks of kindling, and twigs. I managed a defeated sigh. I knew I'd locked all my doors and windows before going to Santa Fe, but obviously, these minor barriers hadn't prevented Ben from getting into the house. I'm not even going to ask, I thought.

"This will please you, White-Hawk woman," he greeted, gesturing toward the open front door.

It will please me that he's letting all the warm air out of the house? I shook my head, waited for him to explain.

"I have cleaned away all evil left by the enemy."

I raised my eyebrows.

"Now that your house is cleansed, you can wash yourself. I have put plenty of amole in your cleaning room."

"What do you mean, Ben?"

"This is important," he continued. "You should wash yourself right away so your enemy's evil doesn't make you sick."

"You mean Luján?"

Ben nodded. "Luján. Yes. Luján the Spanish enemy. He was here before, you know. He was even more of an enemy then."

"Luján? You mean he tried to rob Sam, too?"

"No. I talk about when he came and called himself Governor and brought the Spanish enemy people back. It was the end of our freedom."

Now I was fascinated. I almost forgot about my rented truck and the rugs, new bed, paint, and fabric. "Ben," I said, "I want to hear more about this story. In fact, I'd love to hear all about it. But could you help me carry some things from the truck? Then, I need to return the truck to Santa Fe. Maybe you could ride with me, tell me this story while I drive."

"White-Hawk woman," he said, his tone serious, "I have cleaned all the evil from your house, and I have brought amole for you to clean yourself. If you don't do this now . . ."

"Okay, okay." I could see this wasn't a joke. Ben believed everything he was saying. He believed it so intensely, I was beginning to believe it too.

I left Ben to finish sweeping out the wood bin while I bathed myself with amole. I had no idea what it was. But while I bathed with it, I guessed it was some kind of soap. I really didn't care for it. Afterwards I went into my bedroom, found my new bed in place, set up properly. Very odd. How did he carry these awkward heavy things alone? And why hadn't I heard him moving the furniture through the house?

Next I noticed the pseudo-Navajo rug was on the floor in the bedroom, and the fabric was laying on the mattress. In the living room I found the braided rug spread out on the floor. I'd intended to have them the other way around, but this seemed to suit the rooms, and it suited me. I changed into a fresh sweater and jeans, went to find Ben.

The cans of paint were stacked on the floor in the dining room, and the wood bin was back in its place beside the hearth. Everything was sparkling clean. End of one mystery. I now knew who cleaned the house before I moved in. Not Sam, and not some hired janitor service. Had to be Ben. I was beginning to feel guilty, like I should be paying him for all this work. Maybe that's why he did it. He needed the money.

"Ben," I called out the back door. I waited, but there was no answer. I'll start paying him by the hour, I thought, and I'll pay him for everything he's done up to now.

I drove the truck back to Santa Fe and collected the Honda. But I kept thinking about the story Ben started to tell me. The story about a Spanish enemy named Luján. It occurred to me that if anyone could tell me more about this story, Sam could. Before leaving town I pulled into a convenience store and used the public telephone. Sam's daughter-in-law answered. I told her who I was, asked if Sam was there.

"He took the dog for a walk," she said. "You have a problem with something at the house?"

I could've told her a few stories about Luján. "No," I said, "No problem. I'm here in town...doing some shopping. Just thought I'd stop by for a visit before heading home."

There was a pause on her end, then she said, "I'm sure Sam would appreciate that. You can come on over, but you might have to wait a half hour, or so."

I assured her I didn't mind and she gave me directions to their home.

The house was located in an exclusive section of Santa Fe, and it was impressive. Sam's son—a short, balding man with a heavy beard—greeted me at the door, invited me in.

"You can wait in the library," he said, showing me the way.

The library was a comfortable room with a Ben Franklin fireplace, books from floor to ceiling on two walls, and a large picture window looking out into a garden. The garden appeared to be enclosed in the middle of the house. I guessed the house was styled after original hacienda designs.

I was examining titles on several books, when Sam appeared at the doorway.

"Now ain't this a nice surprise!" he said, crossing the room to give me a hug. I tensed a bit. I wasn't accustomed to being hugged. "Sit, sit," he said, waving at one of two large wing-backed chairs in front of the window.

We talked briefly about the recent weather changes which brought warmer temperatures, about my plans to paint the house, about nothing that really mattered. His daughter-in-law carried in a large silver tray filled with holiday candies and cookies and glasses of pink colored juice. She placed the tray on a table in front of us, and left without saying a word. Sam glanced over at me and grinned. "She's as bad as Nakani," he chuckled. I chuckled, too.

Sam told me to help myself, so I sampled some of the refreshments, and sipped at the pink juice. I was still not sure what it was. After a short time Sam fixed his eyes on me and asked, "When you gonna tell me what you came to see me 'bout, Missy?"

I hesitated, then I told him Luján tried to burglarize my house, but Ben surprised him and he killed himself in an automobile accident while trying to get away. I didn't think it was necessary to alarm Sam about my own mis-adventures with Luján. However, I did tell him Ben said something curious about this Luján being an enemy, like the other one.

I was right, Sam understood what Ben was talking about, and he had a story he was more than happy to share; a story that would explain the mystery about Luján.

"Why, ain't you ever heard 'bout the Pueblo rebellion of 1680?" he asked.

"You tell me about it," I said, settling back into the comfortable chair. "It was real spectac'lar," he said. "Pueblo people all over the southwest got together to plan a kind of revolution against them Spaniards. They came right near to havin' their way, too. These Pueblos—that's what them Spaniards labeled 'em, you know. I already told you that."

I nodded.

"Yeah. Well they'd been hurtin' pretty bad for more'n a century. Oppressed is what they was." He paused to see if I was following. "That's a fancy word for slavery."

"Yes, I know," I said, encouraging him to get on with the story.

"Umhum, well, let's see." He stared out the window and scratched his chin, popped a cookie into his mouth, then continued. "Sometime around 1675, I think it was, them Pueblos realized they had themselves a real powerful leader. Now this fella had what you'd call one helluva lot of charisma. Went by the name of Pope.

"'Bout this same time, one of them Catholic friars—over at San Ildefonso—well he got to be just plain paranoid. Believed some of them Pueblos put a curse on him to make him sick. Result was a bunch got put on trial. Why, more'n forty got sold off like slaves, and 'bout four more got hanged. Now, I ain't gotta tell you, this didn't sit well with these Pueblo people. With a little shove from Pope, them Pueblos sent near a hundred of their principal warriors to that Spanish Governor of Santa Fe's house. They offered this fella chickens, eggs, tobacco, some of their best crops, and some right nice cured skins. They meant to bargain for the let-go of their kinfolks. You can imagine, that governor was fairly intimidated—having near a hundred tough warriors at his door, and he struck a deal right there."

"Where does Luján fit into this story?" I asked.

"Why he's the worst part of it," Sam said. He reached for another cookie and finished the juice in his glass. Then he said, "Worth mentioning I think, so's you'll understand, these same Pueblos'd been trying to free themselves from them Spaniards for more than eighty years. But them Spaniards had real superior fightin' tools. You know, they had some right fine war horses, not to mention their guns and soldiers.

"But I reckon that Pope character put things in a bad light for them Spaniards. Old records say he wasn't just a physically strong warrior, but that he was a genius when it came to smarts—a genuine hero type, you know. But records also have it that he was a medicine man, known and respected beyond them Pueblos. Seems them Navajos, Apaches, and a few others thought highly of Pope's medicine. Now, if you ask me, that superior medicine-man quality prob'ly gave him most of his success."

"What about Luján?" I reminded.

"You just listen," Sam snapped. "Trouble with young people is they don't listen.

"Back to this Pope character. Now he arranged meetin's between all the pueblos, and when he had their trust and backing, he flat out caused an uprisin' that changed the history of New Mexico and Arizona forever. Now, ain't that spectac'lar?"

I nodded.

Sam seemed impressed. "Darned spectac'lar," he repeated. "'Bout twenty thousand Pueblos joined in on this rebellion—sometime in August 1680. Them Spaniards were killed, starved, and driven out of the country. Anything reminding them Pueblos of them Spaniards was destroyed.

"And now, this is real interesting: to clean themselves of any bad influence left by them Spaniards, they had a ceremony, then they all went to the rivers and scrubbed themselves from head to toe with bowls of amole. That's soap-weed."

I smiled, remembering my bowl of soap from Ben.

"Now," Sam said, "Here is what you've been waitin' for. In 1691 Don Diego de Vargas Zapata Luján—them Spaniards did enjoy a mouthful for a name—anyway, he was signed in as governor. Spanish boss's came ridin' in again like a bad dream that wouldn't quit, and the Pueblo peoples just plain lost out."

"You said this happened in 1691? That was three hundred years ago."

"That's right," Sam said. "Three hundred years ago. They never did get their freedom back."

"But," I argued, "that particular Luján lived three hundred years ago."

"These Pueblo people got mighty long memories," Sam grinned.

Sam's daughter-in-law came into the library soon after the story was told and let Sam know it was past his bedtime. I understood the hint, thanked her for the refreshments, and told Sam how much I'd enjoyed hearing about the Pueblo rebellion of 1680.

It was nearly midnight when I got back to my house, but I was a long way from being sleepy. I took the blanket off my sofa, put another log on the fire, then curled up beside the hearth and stared at the flames. Somewhere during the early morning hours before sunrise I fell asleep.

10

The week before Christmas passed without visits from neighbors, or Sam, or any more of the Luján family. When Christmas Eve arrived, I was beginning to wonder if Sam forgot he'd invited me to go with him and Kopeki and Ben to San Felipe, which he referred to as the Christmas Pueblo. I had my doubts at the time, and in all the books I'd read, I didn't see one mention about San Felipe being a Christmas Pueblo.

Didn't matter, I told myself. I'd finished painting the entire interior of the house, and sewed simple but attractive drapes for each window. Now I walked through each room, tested the walls. They were all dry. This day I could hang my drapes.

I stood before one of the living room windows and admired the view. Such a remarkable morning. The heavens sent a flood of sapphire spraying seductively across the sky, then sprinkled this scenic feast with delicious whirling, twirling, dizzy, powdered sugar clouds. There was no place on earth like this. There was no place but this. Just me and my house, nestled safely between soft foothills and ancient mesas, flat topped mountains, and towering rock cliffs.

Just me.

And my neighbors.

Reluctantly I turned away and set about slipping hems through rods which fastened to hooks in the walls. When all the drapes were in place I arranged pleats and gathers and tie backs, and took an easy stroll around, complimenting myself for doing a truly fine job. My house was turning out to be as charming a home as it was a captivating agreeable day.

"It is also a very good day for a cup of coffee," I thought aloud with a chuckle, remembering how Kopeki had said the same thing the day I met him—and his memory. I went to the kitchen, measured Columbian and Java beans into the grinder, then dipped the new grounds into the basket, and retired to the living room to enjoy the aroma while I waited.

While waiting, Kopeki arrived at the back door, announced himself, then he passed through the kitchen, bringing us both a fresh mug of my Columbian-Java brew. I was thinking, he has a good nose.

Kopeki was dressed in what seemed to be more of a costume than an outfit. The baseball hat was gone. Where his hair was usually tied back, it now fell in long silver strands across his small bony shoulders. A bright red bandana circled his forehead and was tied behind. He wore a crisp white cotton shirt. The shirt had long loose sleeves, an open neck, and a square loose hemline. Several necklaces made from shells circled around his neck. Kopeki's trousers were gray, and the most glorious, colorful, woven belt I'd ever seen was tied at his waist, its ends hanging down his back. Varying sizes of rich turquoise and small silver bells were sewn into the belt. On his feet were leather moccasins, while leggings heavily ornamented with bright silver buttons and conchas wrapped his lower legs.

"My-oh-my," I said with a loud sigh. "You certainly cut a striking and picturesque form today!"

"What will this White-Hawk-magician turn into tonight?" he asked, ignoring my compliment. His creviced old face was filled with a grin, and his stubby yellow teeth sparkled. He seemed amused with his question. I had no idea what he meant.

"You going somewhere?" I asked, still checking out the costume.

"We always go to the big dance," he was still smiling.

I wondered out loud, "Could that be the one at the Christmas Pueblo?"

He nodded. "Very good day for more coffee," he said.

I laughed and took his cup to the kitchen for a refill. When I returned, Kopeki had the television on, was watching Saturday morning cartoons. "These are the best Kosh'airi I have seen," he said with a wink, and a gesture at the animated caricatures of a coyote and a roadrunner on the screen.

Kosh'airi, I repeated to myself. I recognized the word from something I'd read in one of the books. Kosh'airi were delight

makers, thought of by some as clowns. But from what I had read,
I didn't believe they were clowns at all. I believed Kosh'airi were
a kind of rule enforcer, a master of the dance ceremony. Their
clownish appearances and sometimes silly antics were part of their
disguise, not their function.

Kopeki was, by now, absorbed in cheering the sneaky coyote
on, advising him how best to snare the roadrunner. I handed him
his coffee, shook my head and went to my bedroom to examine
the clothes in my closet. "Seems there really is a Christmas
Pueblo," I mumbled, trying to guess what I could wear that
would be appropriate.

Ben arrived and joined Kopeki in front of the television. I decided
to ask Ben what women wore to this ceremony. Ben wasn't as dec-
orously attired as Kopeki. A multi colored scarf was tied around
the crown of his head, and he had large silver loops which were
kind of like earrings in his ear lobes. He wore a solid black long
sleeve shirt, and solid black slacks. Around his neck he wore an
enormous, impressive squash blossom necklace, its silver freshly
polished, and its turquoise a light blue. A silver and turquoise
concha belt circled his small waist, and he wore brown buckskin
slipper-type moccasins.

I stepped into the living room and gave a little whistle. "You
boys are really dressing to the nines for this dance," I said.
"Maybe you could give me an idea what women wear."

They tore their eyes from the television long enough to ex-
change curious glances at each other, and they ignored me. I went
back to the closet.

I finally selected a long black wool skirt, a white silk blouse, and
a black silk shawl heavily embroidered with red and yellow
flowers and butterflies. I polished a pair of black high heels,
changed my mind, and slipped my stocking feet into a pair of
sturdy loafers. I didn't know how much walking and standing
we'd be doing, and I wasn't going to chance spraining an ankle in
heels.

When I emerged from my bedroom, both Kopeki and Ben forgot their television program. They stared at me, mouths open and
speechless. I couldn't tell if this was a compliment, or shock. I
smiled at them, went to the kitchen, prepared a basket of sandwiches and a large thermos of coffee. Seemed like the refresh-

ments might come in handy. Then I remembered I owed Ben a lot of money for the chores he'd been doing. I dug into my cash, took out a twenty and several tens, carried this to Ben.

"What is this?" he asked.

"It's payment for all the work you've done for me," I said.

Kopeki gave me a strange look.

"Don't you want to be paid?" I asked.

Ben turned to Kopeki for help.

I didn't know what to say.

Kopeki turned to me. "Why don't you give him something he can enjoy."

I glanced at Kopeki, and Kopeki grinned and winked.

"Okay," I said to Ben, "What would you like instead of money?"

"I would like a horse."

It was my turn to be speechless.

"That would be a good thing for Ben," Kopeki agreed.

At that moment I heard a truck pulling into the yard. It was Sam's truck. Saved by the fossil. I went to the door to greet him. Sam was dressed casually in a new denim jacket, a fresh western style shirt, a turquoise and coral bola tie, creased blue jeans, a cowboy hat, and polished western boots.

We watched television, and visited, until mid-afternoon. No one brought the horse subject up again. I was curious as to when we were going to leave for San Felipe, was about to ask, when I heard quite a stir outside. I went to the window and saw half a dozen people climbing into the back of Sam's truck.

Four were men. I guessed their ages to be between eighteen and forty. Two were women, probably in their early twenties. Hardly old timers, which is the way I remembered Sam first described the people who might go with us. The men were dressed similarly to Kopeki, except one had a wide oval brim hat instead of a scarf or bandana. The women wore black dresses, embroidered on the top and bottom in lavender. Their right shoulders were draped with more black cloth, and their left shoulders were bare. Around their waists they wore bright red and blue woven belts, which tapered off with long fringes. Their lower legs were wrapped round and round with white leather, and their small feet were clad in moccasins. Both wore multiple strands of silver beads and shells around their necks, and their ink black hair was either short, or skillfully tucked and appearing short.

I marveled that no one seemed affected by the chill in the air. Although the snow had melted and the sunshine was thick, the temperature remained steady in the forties throughout the day.

"Will we be leaving soon?" I asked Sam.

"Why? You in a big hurry to go stand in the cold and wait?"

"Well," I said, "Looks like some of Kopeki and Ben's 'old timer' friends are out in your truck. By the way they are dressed, I'd say they plan on going to San Felipe with us. . . ."

11

Sam's truck had a large cab which easily seated Sam, myself,
Ben, and Kopeki. Ben and Kopeki volunteered to sit in the back
after I insisted they offer their places to the two women, but the
women declined. I hoped they wouldn't get cold riding in the
truck's bed, and was glad for the change in weather, glad the sky
was clear and no signs of rain or snow approached from any
direction.

"You know much about the history of San Felipe?" Sam asked
me, shortly after we left my house.

I'd considered myself knowledgeable in most areas of history,
until recently. Recently I was learning there were a lot of things I
didn't know. I mumbled something unintelligible in reply to
Sam's question.

"You know what the Pueblo word for the first village of San Felipe was?" he asked, ignoring my mumbles.

"No."

"What was it, Kopeki?" Sam peered around me at Kopeki,
who sat next to the window.

"Katishtya."

"That's it," Sam said. "Sounds more like what you'd call a
pueblo, now don't you think? San Felipe came from them Spaniards, you know."

"San Felipe is not the right word," Kopeki added his two
cents.

"That's right," Sam said, "it sure ain't. You wanna know who
called it San Felipe, Missy?"

"Sure."

"Place we're headin' ain't even the original site," Sam rambled
off on a new thought. "Where was that first site?" He peered at
Kopeki again.

"In the place of shadows," Kopeki said.

"What he means is, it was at the foot of Tamita Mesa. Well, anyway, what was I talking about?"

"You're telling me who gave San Felipe its name."

"Castaño de Sosa. That's what he called himself. Was passing through this area 'bout 1591. Just up and renames the place. Real arrogant, I'd say. Surprised he didn't call it the pueblo of Castaño de Sosa."

Ben and Kopeki laughed uproariously at Sam's sarcasm.

"Fray Cristóbal de Quiñones," Sam raised his voice over the laughter.

"Who was he?"

"Another one of them Spaniards. He's the one brought Catholicism to San Felipe. 'Course the first church was built in that Tamita Mesa village. One we're going to for tonight's ceremony was built around 1700. Been rebuilt a few times since then."

"You're a bit of an authority on Pueblo history," I commented. "Do you get this from books?"

"He is a very good listener," Kopeki said, "and I am a very good talker."

And I should have figured that out, I thought.

San Felipe was a farther distance than I'd guessed. We drove southeast to Santa Fe, then we headed southwest to the San Felipe Indian Reservation. The pueblo—poised in dignity near the banks of the Rio Grande—was still a good distance from the main highway, and when we reached it, there was an enormous crowd. Automobiles and pickup trucks were parked, in what appeared to be a random plan of chaos, anywhere there was space. The area surrounding the pueblo village was even more congested, with people from all imaginable backgrounds. I saw license plates from Arizona, California, Utah, Colorado, Nevada, Texas, Wyoming, North Dakota, and even Alaska.

Sam bumped the GMC up and down narrow aisles of chrome bumpers, finally parking between a shiny white Cadillac limousine from Bernalillo County, and a dented, dirty yellow Camaro from Cibola County.

"Watch your step, Missy," Sam cautioned as I slid from the cab and tried to keep my feet out of the mud which seemed everywhere. I reached back for the basket of sandwiches and the thermos of coffee. "Might wanna leave that in the truck," he said, "unless you're wantin' to lug it around till your arm falls off."

"How long will we be here?"

"Oh," he scratched his chin, "I reckon we usually leave 'bout four."

I glanced up at the sky. Being winter, night arrived early, but it couldn't have been more than seven o'clock. "You mean four in the morning?" I asked, sure he'd made a mistake.

"'Bout four," he nodded.

"How long will the dances go on?"

"Oh, well," he said with a big smile, "those won't even start up till midnight. We're on Indian time, now, you know."

No, I didn't know. What was Indian time, and how was it different from regular clock time? He stepped around me, reached into the truck, pulled several cartons of cigarettes from beneath the seat. I didn't say anything, tried not to show my curiosity.

Then it occurred to me, Ben and Kopeki were gone. I looked all about, stretched my neck to see over parked vehicles, noticed the six who'd ridden in the truck bed were also missing. "Sam," I said, "where is everyone?"

His wrinkled eyebrows let me know he thought my question was odd. "These are their people, you know," he said. "Only time they all come down from the sacred mountains is when there's a big get-together. Gives 'em a chance to see old friends and relatives. Near as I can tell, these dances are kinda like social parties. Sometimes I've seen lines of ancestors stretching back a thousand years. Real touching, it is. Too bad my relatives don't have parties like this . . . least ways, none I ever knew 'bout. I think I enjoy comin' much as Kopeki and his bunch." Sam paused to adjust his bola tie, loosening it. "Why," he continued, "when my time is up, I think I'll come right back to these parties. I reckon that's what I'll do. Kopeki'll be here, same as Ben, and we'll catch up on our gossip when we meet at your house first to drink up all your coffee."

Now I wrinkled my eyebrows, but Sam simply winked.

We crossed the area used as a parking lot, and were following a hard-packed dirt path into a huge courtyard bordered by village houses. Some of the doors were open, and people wandered in and out, as if this were expected and accepted. Pahos were everywhere. Hundreds, maybe thousands.

"I've got some peace offerin's for some of my friends," he grinned, holding out the cigarettes. His comment reminded me of when I met Kopeki, and our strange little peace-smoke.

"I'll just wander about," I said, sensing I wasn't welcome to follow him around. I didn't know what else to do. I'd never been to a ceremony at a pueblo; I'd never been to any kind of formal Christmas ceremony, either.

Sam seemed to know what I was thinking. He said, "Tell you what I'll do, I'll deliver these, then maybe we can drive on to Albuquerque, see them farolitos lighting up Old Town. That's real spectac'lar. 'Course you'll have to do the drivin' 'cause that's a might stretch of my energy, you know."

The idea sounded pleasing. Farolitos, or luminarias as some called them, were paper bags filled with sand and a candle. I'd seen them at Old Town San Diego once or twice. I remembered how nice they made me feel—although I didn't have a clue as to why anyone would set them out. I'd read that in New Mexico, people set millions of farolitos out all around the state. I believed I'd already seen that many when we passed through Santa Fe.

"What about the ceremony here, and the others?" I asked.

"Well now, that ain't a problem. By the time we go to Old Town, do our walkabout, and drive back here, the dancin' just might be ready to start. As for the others, they're busy lookin' up kinfolks and friends. You couldn't drag 'em away, even if you could find 'em—which I serious doubt."

"You don't think this is all too much for you?" I asked, recalling how early his daughter-in-law announced his bedtime.

"Nah," he said, pausing, then adding, "You're welcome to go with me while I do my rounds."

I hesitated, "No, I'll let you deliver those peace-smokes yourself. Seems to be a few interesting things to watch. Why don't you go on, and meet me back here."

"Good enough. How 'bout in an hour?"

"About an hour," I agreed.

He started to walk away, stopped, and looked back. "You know about peace-smokes?" he asked with a tone of surprise.

I smiled, "From first hand experience."

Sam's truck didn't shift as smoothly as the Ford, and it steered a bit stiff, but I found myself enjoying my view sitting above most of the vehicles on the highway. It made me feel more in control of the traffic while Sam told me which road to take, and when to turn right or left.

In spite of the heavy holiday traffic, our drive didn't last long. Albuquerque was less than an hour from San Felipe. Old Town Albuquerque was surprisingly similar to Old Town San Diego. The layout of the buildings seemed identical, and the structures looked the same. If I hadn't known this was New Mexico, I'd have sworn we were in San Diego, California. Probably same Spanish reasoning was plastered into both—after all, they were early Spanish settlements.

"Ever seen farolitos pretty as this?" Sam asked.

I don't remember if I answered, I was too busy admiring the illuminated bags which were everywhere. They lined sidewalks and roads, small adobe fences and high walls, roof tops and store fronts, church steeples and courtyards, and every walkway in or around Old Town.

I was inching along in traffic, looking for any space large enough to park the truck, when two policemen on horseback emerged from a side road and flagged my lane to a stop. A few seconds later a bus crossed in front of us, and then another, and another. I'd counted twenty-five already.

"Tour bus," Sam said.

"Must be one heck of a business. They all look full."

"Yeah. They fill 'em up over at the shopping malls, then drive around Albuquerque. This is their highlight. I doubt most of 'em are tourists. Prob'ly live right here in town, but don't wanna mess with traffic and huntin' up a parkin' spot."

"I don't believe we're going to find a parking spot," I said.

"I know where to park," Sam said. "Soon as these monster wagons get out of the way, I'll show you."

Sam directed me to the almost empty parking lot behind the Sheraton Hotel, across the street from Old Town. While we crossed the street, the tour bus parade was heading back. I started to run for the sidewalk, but Sam continued at his leisurely pace. The buses had to stop for him. When he reached the sidewalk I noticed the grin on his face, but didn't comment.

Later we joined a small group of strangers in a walk around the square.

"Isn't this lovely?" a woman with an English accent said.

"Sure is," Sam was happy to reply. She moved through our little crowd and walked at his side. I thought, he's a natural charmer. I stepped back to make room for her, and found myself in stride with a couple about my age.

"My feet are frozen," the woman complained to the man.

"Walk faster," he said, "and they'll warm up."

"I'm walking as fast as that old geezer ahead can go," she snapped, indicating Sam with a nod of her head. Sam was too busy listening to the English woman to hear the insult.

"He's my grandfather," I said, enjoying the surprised embarrassment on her face. My lie was well spent. The couple fell behind, and I was now walking next to a woman in her sixties, and a younger woman, and a teenage boy.

The younger woman kept saying "Mother, did you see that?" I would glance around, never sure what she intended her mother to see.

Then, while our group paused to admire the farolitos which climbed the old mission walls, bordered the roof, and dotted the steeple, the teenage boy said, "Mother, if you'd shut up, Grandmother might be able to enjoy herself."

The woman huffed and stomped her feet to stay warm. Already ice was forming where melted snow made puddles around the courtyard. I eased carefully through the group until I was next to Sam. The English woman was still talking. I don't think she even slowed her words to inhale. But Sam looked happily entertained. I hated to butt in. "Sam," I said. "It's really getting late. Hadn't we better start for San Felipe?"

12

As I feared, the highway was icy, especially crossing bridges. We reached San Felipe without skidding off the road—not because of my expert driving skills, but because Sam's truck had good tires, good traction, and held steady. We ate several sandwiches from the basket, and drank most of the coffee.

"Kopeki'll be a might upset," Sam chuckled, peering into the thermos. He replaced the cap, slipped it under the seat, and took a nap. I woke him when we were safely parked near the pueblo.

"Dancers goin' at it yet?" he asked, rubbing his eyes.

"I don't think so," I whispered—then wondered why I was whispering. In a normal voice I said, "I can't hear a thing, and I don't see too many people." Gesturing at the cars I added, "Seems like they've got to be around...somewhere."

"Must be midnight," Sam said, climbing down from the cab. "C'mon. We'd better get over to the church."

He acted like this was all familiar, so I followed.

Suddenly I sensed things were changing. The earth was changing. There was a Spirit of change, and it was more powerful than anything I'd ever experienced before. I thought, is this religion, or what? I decided it was, and that what I was feeling came from all these religious people. This was their experience; they allowed me to share it.

Our steps carried us nearer to the church. On every side people were coming and going from houses. The opening and closing of doors caused light to spray across the ground, bounce off adobe fences, then disappear, lost, concealed by night shadows.

And now village doors began to open again, and everywhere people emerged. They walked to the ends of paths, floated across the courtyard—ghostlike—wrapped in their shawls and blankets, and stopped in the adobe walled plaza before the quiet church. In the candle bright darkness I could see spectators standing around the perimeter in pairs and groups, their eyes fixed on the church. It had two bell-tower steeples, one on either side, a raised facade across the top, with a cross in the middle. Above the double doors was a balcony with wooden railing. And behind the church, drenched in starlight, Black Mesa rose to the right in the shape of a rounded hill; to the left a canyon dipped momentarily, meeting the foothills of a flat-topped mesa beyond this. There were no trees and precious few shrubs growing on these dirt mesa mounds. I imagined this place would be uncomfortable and disagreeable when the wind blew, stirring up all that dirt.

Then the church doors flew wide and a brightness from inside lit up the plaza. We passed through, and found ourselves standing shoulder to shoulder amidst an assortment of people. Candles burned brightly. There were no benches or seats, only hard clay dirt beneath our feet. What kind of a church is this, I wondered.

Sam read my mind. He whispered into my ear, "It's an Indian church." Of course, I thought. I should know that.

While we stood there—waiting for what, I didn't know— people kept entering the church. I couldn't imagine it would hold more, but they came until every space was filled. Then, people walked single file toward the manger to view their Christ. Gifts were in the crib. I was curious about everything, and dying to ask Sam to explain. But I took my cue from the crowd's silence.

A short time later Mass was said. When it was finished the priest and a few others left. Everyone began pushing tightly against the walls, clearing the middle of the church. Now I heard drums sending their message from somewhere off in the distance outside—a steady cadence of beating. This seemed to signal the unusual birdlike noises which carried down from the choir loft. I glanced up and saw dozens of children creating the sounds with an instrument.

"Bird warblers," Sam whispered in my ear. "Them little boys makes 'em all themselves."

I watched with amazement, mesmerized by this unusual, beautiful ceremony, forgetting the drumbeats, until they were suddenly at the church doors. The birdsongs continued and the drummer came in and moved quickly to the cleared area. A chorus of singers followed, and when they were inside, a dancer entered. He wore heavy silver with turquoise and coral inlays, a costume sewn from leather, feathers, and shells, and I was reminded of Kopeki's "lost boy" story. I wondered if these were eagle feathers. My wandering thoughts were reined in, and I watched with full attention, while the man moved gracefully about the open space. He stooped to caress the ground, then rose to stretch his arms high, repeating this over and over, keeping time with the steady chants from his singers.

Afterwards a group of women entered the church. They had odd black headdresses which seemed to balance on their heads easily. "Them's mantas," Sam whispered, pointing at the headdresses, "and the stuff they're holding onto is spruce. They call spruce 'hakak.' It's real sacred, you know. Spruce. They're believin' it gave 'em eternity. Use spruce to make their ladders leadin' out of them kivas. Kinda like climbin' the sacred ladder out from the underworld, you know."

I nodded and smiled, hoped he'd be quiet. People nearby were staring at us, letting us know this was a time for silence from the spectators.

The male dancer continued to dance, and now the women were following him in a single file line. I marveled at all the turquoise jewelry the women wore. Each one must've had several pounds of it on her body. The extra weight didn't affect their graceful shuffling, which they kept up without missing a beat.

Eventually the dancers left the church in the same order they entered. Next the drummers left. And we, the spectators, were left standing in our awe, listening to the birdsongs which the children continued to create with their warbler instruments. "Right spectac'lar," Sam sighed.

Then, just when I thought the ceremony was finished, a second drum sounded at the door. I turned to see dancers dressed to represent deer—with antlers, masks, deerskin, and canes in their front hands to imitate front legs. One of the dancers was dressed to look silly. I guessed he was their delight-maker, their clown. They began to dance in a prancing fashion, through the church, out of the church, into the plaza. When they were gone, the first dancers returned to offer prayers. Later, each group of dancers returned to offer prayers. This part of the ceremony lasted a long time.

Finally, when I was too absorbed to think of time, Sam said in a normal voice, "It's four o'clock. We're goin' to be the last to leave if we don't get a move on."

I glanced to my sides, and behind. The church was nearly empty and all the dancers were gone. "Wow," I gasped. "That was spectacular indeed."

Sam was leading the way through the plaza—beyond the courtyard and the village paths, to the waiting truck—when I remembered my neighbors. Then I saw them. Kopeki, Ben, and the other six. They were sitting in the truck bed, talking excitedly about the Christmas event, having a very good time.

I drove everyone back to my house. Made several pots of coffee, and tried to talk Sam into resting before he returned to Santa Fe.

"No," he argued. "I take 'em to these dances all the time. First time someone else did the drivin'. I'm right rested, and I'll be gettin' on to my son's house."

When Sam left, the others left, too. I took a hot bath, wrapped up in a warm flannel robe, put a fresh fire in the fireplace, and sat in my good chair, waiting for the sun to come up. It wouldn't be long, now.

13

My neighbors had not been to visit for several days, I hadn't heard from Sam, and I guessed everyone was busy with their holidays. I had my house to myself, most of my major chores were complete, and I decided it was time to begin a few ceramic projects. First I would need a couple gallons of slip, an assortment of interesting plaster molds, and some tools for cleaning greenware. I'd also need a gallon of clear glaze and about half a dozen small jars of ceramic paint. Of course, I had planned on tackling real clay, but why stress myself? It was so much easier to pour molds.

I'd forgotten what day of the week it was, and had to switch the television on for a while to find out: Wednesday. Regular Wednesday. Not a legal holiday Wednesday.

Plenty of stores would be open in Santa Fe, and I knew I could find everything I needed.

I was locking up the house, though I knew it was a waste of time, when I heard a woman's voice. I couldn't understand what language she spoke, but it wasn't English, and it wasn't Spanish. I turned around to face her.

She was short, probably five feet tall at the most, and stout. Not that she was obese, but she was by no means fragile. Her black hair was tied behind her thick neck, and her body was draped with a very unattractive sack dress. I thought she might be trying to make up for the dress by overdoing it with her jewelry. She wore half a dozen necklaces of silver beads, coral, and turquoise; her wrists and waist displayed bands with multicolored shells woven into the fabric. Her feet were clad in moccasins and leggings similar to the ones the women had worn the day we went to San Felipe. It was hard to guess her age, but she appeared younger than me. Early thirties at the most.

"I'm sorry," I said, "I didn't understand you. Do you speak English, or even Spanish?"

"Ahg!" She spit on the ground several times. "Spanish! Ahg!" And then she spit some more. Seemed she didn't care for Spanish.

"English, then?" I asked. I detected a twinge of humbleness in my voice. She was small, but she had a tendency to make me feel intimidated.

Me? Intimidated. Now that was a rare occasion!

"Here," she said, throwing a handful of cornmeal on my door-step and forcing a bowl of water into my hands. "Cajete." She watched me. I had no idea what she meant.

"Cajete," she said, raising her voice, slapping at the bowl of water.

"Cajete," I repeated, recognizing I was holding this cajete thing.

"For you," she said.

"Thank you." I was confused; my thanks insincere.

"You are White-Hawk woman, keeper of this ground." She gestured all around to include my property and house.

I nodded.

"I am kai-iddeh," she said, "wife of the head medicine man."

I stared at her. I didn't know whether to invite her in, or hide. I wished I had a few cigarettes. I remembered my first meeting with Kopeki. Our peace smoke bound us, forbid us to make trouble for each other. This woman looked like she could make trouble.

"Kai-iddeh!" she repeated with intention.

"Oh, okay," I said. "Your name is Kai-iddeh. Yes. That's a lovely name."

She stared at me with an expression that bordered on disgust. "Why do you make jokes? My name is Nakani! I am kai-iddeh!" She was beating her broad chest, "Wife of the head medicine man! Husband is Kopeki!"

Okay, I might be slow, but I was beginning to understand. Kai-iddeh was the word meaning 'wife of the head medicine man.' Now I was having trouble believing she was Kopeki's wife. She could have been his granddaughter. Because of the things Sam had said, I imagined she would be quite elderly. And I hadn't been told by anyone that Kopeki was a head medicine man. I pictured him in my living room, enchanted by the cartoon story of sneaky coyote forever trying to capture clever roadrunner. A medicine man? Kopeki? Very hard to believe.

"Would you like to come in?" I asked. Little miss trouble wasn't going away.

I was removing my key, getting ready to unlock the door. "No," she said, "I'm going with you. Where are we going?"

I stood there, holding my cajete, trying to assimilate these new bits of information, and feeling like a child who was getting bossed around by a woman who was younger. Already I didn't like Nakani. "I'll just go inside and leave this bowl of water somewhere safe," I said. "Couldn't very well take it with us, could we?" I chuckled.

She stared at me, as if I were truly dense. "It is cajete! Sacred water! You drink it!"

I peered into the clay bowl, noticed it wasn't very clean. Nakani fixed her beady little eyes on me; her expression was stern, if anything. What would she do if I didn't drink it? Grab my jaws and pry them open? Force it down my throat? I could believe she would do that. Slowly I raised the water to my lips, sipped it cautiously, tried not to frown or foam at the mouth. It tasted like sour water. My stomach started to spasm and I thought I might vomit, but I convinced myself these things were all psychological. I pretended to sip some more; I flunked psychology. My key found the lock quickly and my feet raced to the kitchen. I poured the stuff down the drain, rinsed my mouth, and the bowl. Before going back outside I brushed my teeth with salt and gargled with peroxide.

Nakani was waiting in the passenger seat of my Honda. I switched on the radio and set the volume high enough to discourage her from talking. It didn't work. Her voice had volumes the radio couldn't aspire to reach. I'd found one neighbor I could do without.

"Thought I would be a puff of smoke when I died," she yelled.

I tried to concentrate on the blaring radio.

"Or maybe one of them." She pointed at several cumulus clouds overhead. "Or one of those." Now she was pointing at a wind blown cirrus cloud.

I rolled my eyes and shook my head. No wonder Sam's wife couldn't stand her. I could see Nakani bursting into Sam's house, ordering Sam to keep the fire going while she disappeared for a few days to dream up his son's very original name. I wondered why Sam's wife hadn't thrown her out. Wait a minute! This woman wouldn't have been born then. This woman wouldn't have been born for another thirty years!

"Who are you?" I asked over the music.

"What? Can't hear you."

I switched the radio off. "Who are you?"

"I know about magicians," she said. "Trying to trick me. Kopeki said you would do this. But I know you. 'Sometimes White-Hawk woman is like Kosh'airi. She is saying one thing, meaning another.' Kopeki said this. He tells me you are one of the Yahahnas who can't decide to be good or bad. He tells me you can turn into the white hawk and fly away if we don't please you. I brought you cajete. Ben gives you eggs, keeps your house clean. Kopeki allows you his company. You should be very pleased with us."

"Nakani," I said, "do you have a mother, or a grandmother, maybe an aunt. . . somebody with the same name?"

"No. Why? Is this an offensive name?"

"Not really." I thought for a few minutes, decided Sam might have confused people in his recollection. Maybe Kopeki had one wife then, and now he was married to this woman. Poor Kopeki.

"I think I'll tell you about my death," Nakani said.

Your what? I didn't express my surprise, because now I was believing this woman was a nut case. Didn't matter. I was stuck with her for the duration of our Santa Fe excursion, so I might as well listen. Might learn something.

"Death came quickly. One morning I woke up and went outside my house. 'Come and see the new day,' I told Kopeki. But he didn't hear me. When I went to wake him, I could see myself still sleeping beside him. I touched my face and it was cold, my skin was stiff. I had become only the spirit. I sat down and waited for my husband. When he awoke he was very upset. He shook my body for a long time. I kept telling him, 'Your wife is not a live person any more.'

"It was a busy day for my village. My sisters bathed me and painted my arms and legs with broken white lines. Then they washed my hair with yucca soap and combed it dry. Kopeki came in and put a prayer feather in my hair, and he tied prayer feathers to my hands and feet. He also put a prayer feather on my breast, then he left. My sisters put corn pollen into my hands and tied them closed. Then they rubbed corn pollen on my face. Kopeki returned again, this time placing a white mask over my face. It was a rain cloud mask, and helped the spirit people know my village people needed rain.

"Later in the day some more relatives made a grave for my body while my husband stood on the highest terrace and spoke prayers for me. My body was tied to poles, with my knees bent, and I was carried to my grave. A bowl of water was poured over me because I was now a u'wannami, a rain-maker.

"Back in the village piñon fires burned everywhere to help clean away my death... and because smoke makes clouds, and clouds bring rain, and now I was a u'wannami.

"I went first to the north to pay respect to my ancestors; next I went west to Wenimats, land of the perfect mountains and home for some kachinas. Then I went to the great lake where Shipapu can be found..."

"Wait," I interrupted her story.

"I am talking," she said, her tone scolding.

"What's this place beside the lake?"

"Shipapu?"

I nodded.

She wrinkled her nose and squinted severely. More to herself than me she said, "This White-Hawk woman enjoys trick questions. Now she pretends not to know the name for the place where all our people first emerged from the underworld, where they crawled out as naked babies, and sat in the darkness. Then our great mother, Iyatiku, made them sit quietly with their eyes eastward, forcing the sun to emerge and bring light. Why does she pretend not to know this? I think she tests me, to see if I remember..."

I interrupted her again, "Iyatiku?"

"Iyatiku," her voice showed impatience, "is Great Mother Who Judges Her Children. You be silent and listen! Where was I?"

"Great Mother..."

"Yes, yes. Now, Great Mother Iyatiku was there, and she told me I could remain forever in the perfect mountains of Wenimats."

I couldn't hide my skepticism any longer. "Which mountains are those?"

"They are here," Nakani said.

I looked at my surroundings. "What? All these mountains?" I looked out the car at the enormous Sangre de Cristo Range which stretched across north-central New Mexico.

"These are the sacred mountains," Nakani said. "Home to the sacred trees and animals and lakes."

"You believe your people live here? I mean, after they die? You believe the ghosts of all your ancestors live here?"

"Not all," she said. "Iyatiku doesn't let everyone come here. Sometimes Iyatiku thinks a person was evil, and she sends them to the oven of eternal fire, or she makes them stand forever in the circle of shells."

"Sounds like hell."

"Hell," Nakani laughed, "is where all Spaniards must go when they are dead."

"Don't think too much of them, do you?"

Nakani spit on my Honda's floor mat. I didn't want her to do that again, so I kept silent for a few miles. Then she said, "Kopeki's people traveled from a distant village. When they died they had to return to Koh-thlou-wah-la-wah for their judgement."

"Stop, already! They went where when they died?"

She raised her voice and shouted, "Koh-thlou-wah-la-wah! They went to Koh-thlou-wah-la-wah!" She stared at me as if she thought I were a very dense magician.

"I heard what you called it. But where is it?"

Her expression went blank and she sighed heavily, shaking her head. Softly she said, "It is where Kopeki's people go when they die."

"So, it's a place like heaven," I said. Nakani only shrugged. Now I was thinking about what she said, about a different village. "What's the name of the village Kopeki came from?" I asked.

"Hawikuh." She paused to see if I were going to interrupt again. When she was satisfied I wouldn't, she added, "Close by was Halona, another village. The enemy who called himself Antonio de Espejo decided to name this other place Zuni. It isn't a word Kopeki knew, but we go there anyway, when it's time for Hai-a-tassi. For Kopeki it is time for Kwashi'amme. For you it is time for November. They offer a ceremony for Shalako and Kopeki visits his ancestors." She paused, eyed me cautiously like a child caught in a lie, and added, "Oh, and we especially like the big feast. Kopeki's ancestors can make a feast better than anyone."

"Shalako," I repeated. "The walking gods? I believe that's what Sam called them. Ten feet tall, I hear. That's a very big kachina."

"Not so big. Just tall."

I nodded. We were entering the north end of Santa Fe, and I was beginning to enjoy this newest neighbor. . . much as I hated to admit it.

14

We drove through town, stopped at two art supply stores, and I didn't find what I was looking for until I had almost given up. It was a warehouse building near St. Vincent Hospital called Pepper's Pottery. Inside I found shelf after shelf filled with ceramic paints and glazes, and in the back I discovered a barn sized room with hundreds of rows of ceramic greenware and all imaginable sizes and shapes of molds.

Nakani gave me a shock by keeping quiet the whole while. She followed, not more than four feet behind, everywhere I went, and her curious eyes studied, consumed, every item she looked at. Two or three times I caught people staring at her clothes, which seemed rude. I would turn and stare back at them, return their rudeness. Nakani watched me carefully, then giggled when the offenders blushed with embarrassment.

It wasn't until I'd filled my cart with an assortment of plaster molds, two gallons of slip, and over a dozen colors of glaze and paint, that the excitement began.

"What? What are you doing?" a woman yelled.

I swung around in time to see Nakani shoving the woman away from one of three shelves filled with small figures of ceramic kachinas. The woman tried to reach over Nakani's head to get one of the figures. Nakani pushed her again. The woman stepped back, hesitated, then punched Nakani in the shoulder. Nakani grabbed the woman's hair and yanked it back until the woman was on the floor. Now both were cursing and screaming while they punched it out, wrestling in the narrow dusty aisle.

Not knowing what caused the fracas, I simply stood and watched, my mouth open and my eyes fixed on the feuding duo.

"Hey! Stop that! You'll disrupt that shelf!" a middle aged man who I presumed was the manager yelled.

Too late. The feuding ladies tumbled into the nearest shelf holding the kachina figures, the shelf tilted and rained ceramic greenware across the aisle. Kachinas crashed, smashed, and shattered
on the concrete floor. Nakani maintained a tight grip on the woman's hair with one hand, and used her free hand like a pommel on
the woman's head.

"Just look at this mess! Look at this! Look at it!" the man kept
yelling. By now everyone in the store was standing behind me
and we were all looking at the mess. He yelled some more, and
we spectators sighed and nodded. The feud on the floor wasn't
letting up. I was sure I didn't want anyone to know Nakani was
with me. It appeared the broken ceramics were going to cost
somebody a lot of money.

"That's enough!" the man ordered. "This is going to stop right
now!" He forced himself between the women and intercepted a
few rough punches, which he took unexpectedly on the jaw. He
grabbed Nakani's elbow, and held tight onto the other woman's
wrist.

"You are no better than a goat's droppings!" Nakani cursed.

"A goat's what!?" the woman struggled, but the man held her
with a firm determination.

"Would someone like to tell me what this outrageous behavior
is about?" he demanded.

Nakani frowned but said nothing.

The woman shouted and pointed at Nakani, saying, "I have
no idea! But I do know that bitch is crazy!"

"Wait! Hold it! No more name calling. Now, calmly, please.
Would one of you ladies explain what happened, before I call the
police and let you explain to them?"

If Nakani could've shot daggers with her glare, the other woman
would've been history. Neither was eager to defend themselves.

"I mean it," the man persisted. "Either you tell me what
caused this mess, or I will phone the police."

"She is a witch!" Nakani spit and grabbed for the woman.

"A what? Why you . . ."

The man's face was red and growing redder. I tried to disappear into the crowd of curious customers.

"White-Hawk woman!" Nakani called.

"What's that?" the other woman snapped. "What's that you
called me?"

The man tried to sound calm. He turned to the watchers and asked, "Does anyone know these women?"

"White-Hawk woman!" Nakani called again.

I emerged slowly from the crowd, nodded my head.

"Who started this?" the man asked me.

I shook my head and shrugged.

"Which of these ladies do you know?"

I pointed at Nakani.

Nakani cast a quick look in my direction, whispered loudly, "This is a good time to make this witch disappear! Go on, White-Hawk woman, make this witch disappear."

"That's it!" the other woman shrieked and grabbed at Nakani's necklaces. The man struggled to hold her back.

"Listen, lady," the man said to me, "I'm gonna offer you the deal of your life. You agree to take your friend here," he nodded his head at Nakani, "and leave my store, and never, ever come back, and I won't call the police."

I stepped forward and took hold of Nakani's other elbow, pulled her to her feet.

"Zap her!" Nakani whispered to me.

"Zap her?"

"Now," Nakani insisted, "zap her now before she switches the corn maidens."

"What corn maidens?"

"There."

My eyes followed her pointing finger to the yet intact shelf of ceramic kachinas. "What? You mean you nearly killed this woman over those?"

The spectators inched closer, trying to hear what Nakani whispered to me, while the manager and the woman on the floor stood up, brushed dust off their clothes.

I groaned and closed my eyes.

"Quick," Nakani urged, "before it's too late!"

"We're going to discuss this in the car," I whispered, then I directed all my attention to the woman who now steadied herself beside the manager. "Lady," I said, "you can consider yourself zapped."

"Well, I never..."

Nakani shrieked with glee, and we quickly made our way to the exit—without any of my slip, molds, or paints.

As we were leaving the parking lot, I said, "So tell me what happened...and please, explain so's I can understand."

"She was trying to switch the corn maidens," Nakani said.

"Some of the ceramic figures were corn maidens. I understand that part, but how could she switch them? And what would she switch them with?"

"There are good corn maidens, and bad corn maidens. Like much rain, no rain. Good weather, storm weather. Everything has a twin. Everything has its opposite."

"Well," I said, "we certainly couldn't have her getting them mixed up then, could we?" As usual, I didn't know what Nakani was talking about.

I could see her studying me. Eventually she said, "You could have turned into a white hawk and blinded her with your claws. Then she couldn't see the maidens, and she wouldn't have known which ones to switch."

Now why hadn't I thought of that?

We drove out of town on the highway that would take us home. I wasn't in the mood to search for another ceramic store. I wasn't sure I would ever be in the mood to do that again—certainly not if this neighbor came along.

Maybe I was learning to dislike her again. Maybe I was learning to dislike her intensely. Or maybe I simply felt sorry for her. I'd decided she didn't have both oars in the water.

We were about fifteen miles north of Santa Fe when Nakani spoke up. "You should bring some more seeds for the Kopishtaiya."

"Why? Who are they?"

"You have met them."

"Really? Where?"

"Is this a trick?" she asked.

I shook my head.

"You are a very good magician," she laughed. "I can never decide if you mean what you say, or if you mean the opposite."

I thought, what does that make me? Good neighbor, or bad neighbor, or the neighbor who can't make up her mind?

"Seriously," I said. "Who am I supposed to get seeds for?"

"Kopeki tells me you have named these Kopishtaiya 'Rooster and his Happy Hens.'"

"Oh! You mean the chickens!" I slowed the Honda, pulled off

the highway, and asked, "Are the chickens out of food already?"

"Rooster and his Happy Hens would like some more seeds," Nakani said. "This time I think they would like corn seeds."

I turned the Honda around and headed back to Santa Fe. I wished Nakani could've mentioned this small item before we were half way home.

I stopped at a feed supply, ordered Nakani to wait in the Honda, and purchased two fifty-pound bags of corn. While I paid the clerk, it occurred to me: Sam bought the feed for Ben's chickens. I recalled the story he'd shared about the horse Ben had kept in the pueblo ruins, until its owner sent the county animal control officers after it. And I also recalled, Ben thought I should get him a horse of his own, and Kopeki agreed. I was glad I didn't agree. The cost to feed chickens was surprisingly expensive. I imagined it must be many times higher to feed a horse.

15

We were less than two miles from the turnoff to my house when we spotted the large animal laying at the side of the highway.

"What in the world!" I gasped, hit the brakes, and came to a stop on the highway shoulder.

"What is it?" Nakani asked, staring at the animal.

"Looks like a horse."

We both crawled out of the Honda and ran to where it lay, but we were too late to help. Blood trickled from its nostrils, and its mouth gaped open, its tongue protruding.

"This is not a horse," Nakani said.

"No. But it's close. It's a mule."

I was shaken by the large creature's demise, and saddened by the thought of someone hitting it with a car, then leaving it there like something discarded and worthless. Certainly its animal spirit had value. I placed my hand on the mule's large head, sensed it was still warm. "Must've just happened. Look how fresh and fluid the blood is."

Nakani bent over the mule, touched the blood on its nose, and nodded. "We can bury it," she suggested.

"You and me? I doubt we could even drag it a foot away from this spot. I think we should drive to that market we passed a few miles back and I'll call the sheriff, let him take care of it." I was thinking about the sheriff who arrived at María's house the day Luján killed himself. I wouldn't mind dumping a problem of this size in his lap. Serve his smart attitude, I thought with a smirk.

Just when we were climbing into the Honda, a sheriff's car pulled up behind us. Nakani glanced at me and said, "You have strong magic, bringing your sheriff so quick." She snapped her fingers on the word 'quick.'

I ignored her, and only rolled my window down when the

familiar uniform sauntered up alongside the car. "You hit that animal?" he asked.

I knew he remembered who I was, but he pretended not to recognize me. I still didn't have New Mexico license plates for the Honda. He didn't say anything about the plates. "No, I didn't hit that animal. Small car like this would probably be destroyed after an impact with something big as a mule, don't you imagine?"

He feigned indifference to my remark and sauntered over to where the unfortunate creature lay. Nakani looked at me questioningly. I made a motion for her to stay in the car. After walking around the mule two or three times, bending to examine injuries where it had been hit, and jotting some things into his notebook, the sheriff returned to my side of the Honda. "You think you could stay until the truck gets here to haul the mule away?"

I shook my head. "I didn't kill the animal," I said. "Can't see it's my responsibility." I rolled my window up, started my engine, signaled—although there was no other traffic on the highway—and pulled away from the scene, headed home. When I glanced in my rearview mirror, the sheriff was watching while we disappeared down the road. I almost thought I saw disappointment in his expression.

First thing I saw when I turned into my driveway was Sam's GMC. Second thing I saw was the mule. Same mule. I could've swore it was the same mule. Except this one was standing next to Sam's truck, tied there by a short piece of rope. Sam was sitting in the cab.

"What's going on?" I asked, jumping out of the car and hurrying toward the mule. I touched it, patted it, made sure I wasn't imagining it. Sam crawled down from the cab.

"Whataya mean?" he asked.

"Sam, we saw a mule that looked exactly like this one—down the road about a mile or more. Someone hit it . . . it was dead."

"Oh, that," he said. Sam smiled and nodded a greeting at Nakani, who was now standing next to the mule, patting its soft muzzle.

"You saw it?"

"Saw the fella that hit it."

"What happened?"

"The animal was tryin' to cross the highway. I was comin' out to see if Ben's chickens needed some more grain."

"I've got two sacks of feed in the car."

"Corn," Nakani added with a wink.

"Corn?" Sam grinned, "Corn'll be a right nice treat. A might on the expensive side..."

"What about the mule?" I asked.

"Oh. Well, I guess it's for Ben."

"Not this one. The dead one."

"Both the same," Sam said.

I didn't say anything for a few minutes. Then I said, "Forget about this mule. Tell me about the dead one."

"Like I said..."

I knew what he was going to say. I interrupted and repeated, "I only want to hear about them one at a time. What happened on the highway?"

"Mule was tryin' to get t'other side," Sam said. "I could see him up there ahead. Truck in front of me hit him. Tried to brake, but it was haulin' a load of alfalfa hay. Fella pulled t'side of the road, so I stopped to help him drag the animal off the blacktop. Big fella—the one that hit the mule. He managed to get it over without much help from me."

"Why didn't you get a veterinarian?"

"Mule was gone. Fella hit him broadside. Right busted up its insides, I reckon."

I sighed heavily, feeling sad about the dead mule, wondering where Sam got the one tied to his truck. I was afraid to ask who would have to buy its feed.

"Ben wants a horse real bad," Sam said. "Mules are part horse, you know. Why, today, when I came up on that situation there on the highway, I figured it'd work out real fine. I figured I'd invite this lost fella," he scratched the mule's big ears, "to come here. His home's with your neighbors, now." Sam grinned and nodded in Nakani's direction. "Ben'll look out for him. Like he does with the chickens, you know. Ought to work out just fine. Kinda like a horse, a mule is, you know."

"Was this one with the other one?" I asked.

"Nope. Same mule."

Sam's a sneaky old fossil, I thought. I knew what he was up to. He was pretending this was the ghost of the dead mule. I knew better. This one was probably tagging along behind the other one, was lucky not to be similarly retired. Why argue? Ben would never forgive me if I let this mule go. Darn that Sam! I was going to be stuck buying the feed. Unless the animal had an owner, like the horse.

Nakani said, "This animal is better than the horse Ben found."

"Why's that?" I asked.

"The horse was of this world."

"So's the mule."

"Not this mule," Sam said, "not anymore."

"If you say so," I said. I didn't want to get into a philosophical discussion with the old fossil. Let him have his game. "Now," I said, "I think we should figure out whose house this animal is going to be staying at. As you can see," I gestured wide, "I don't have a stable."

Nakani looked questioningly at Sam.

"Dana, my dear," Sam said, his tone was uncharacteristically condescending. "Mule here ain't fixin' to be goin' nowhere. Ain't got nowhere to go, except maybe up into them there sacred hills when he's of a mind to have a wander."

"Oh yeah? What if he has a mind to wander out across that highway?"

"Don't make no difference now. Nakani, whataya figure we ought to call this fine animal?"

Nakani's face assumed a pensive expression while she considered the question. After a short time she raised her eyes to Sam and said, "Mule!"

"Almost as original as Sam Junior," I muttered.

"What's that?" Sam asked.

I shook my head, "Nothing. Mule's a real good name. Fits him very well." I slapped my hand on the animal's shoulder.

"Sure does," Sam said. "Nakani here's got a reg'lar talent for findin' the right name."

I listened for any hint of humor in Sam's words, but he appeared entirely serious, as did Nakani.

"Okay," I said. "So whose house is Mule going to stay at? Nakani, do you have a stable at your place? Seems to me if Ben wants to keep this animal, he should keep it at his house."

Nakani turned to Sam and asked, "What does the White-Hawk woman mean?"

"She don't mean a thing," he winked, "she's just playin' some of them magician tricks on us. Ain't no reason Mule here can't stay anywhere he wants." Sam winked at Nakani again. "Like them chickens," he continued. "Remember when they showed up? Remember how they just up and took to them old ruins 'round the courtyard?"

Nakani nodded.

"Yeah, well, Mule here'll roam around till he figures out where he's comfortable."

"Wait one damned minute!" I interrupted. "Tell me you're not serious. You really plan on letting this...Mule...decide for himself? Sam, there are a few holes in your logic."

"Ssshhh," Sam hushed at me. "You're insultin' Mule."

16

Mule stayed. Without stable, fence, or cattle guard, he remained within the boundaries of my property, except for an occasional wandering down the hill to the pueblo ruins. Rooster and the Happy Hens tolerated him as long as he stayed out of their court-yard during feeding time.

Feeding time. Of course, this was a new issue. I returned to the feed store at Santa Fe the same day Mule arrived, purchased several fifty pound sacks of livestock grain, and was advised, "Mules need alfalfa, too."

How was I supposed to get bales of alfalfa into the Honda?

"We can haul it out to you," the store clerk said. "It'll cost you thirty cents a mile—you pay for the truck's return trip as well."

"I've got a better idea," I said. I wrote down Sam's phone number. "This man's going to pick up ten bales for me. You give him a call when those bales are ready."

"Ready anytime," the clerk said.

I grinned. "So call him now."

"You gonna pay?"

I shook my head. "Let him pay."

"Whatever," the clerk said.

As the weeks passed, I learned to accept Mule's presence and odd behaviors—like the way he stood outside my living room window every time the television was on and tried to peer through. Mule was entertained with Kopeki's choice of programs, but he usually grunted and snorted at the things I enjoyed viewing. Sometimes it could get distracting—all that grunting and snorting which I knew was deliberately timed. But I pretended not to notice, and stub-bornly pulled my chair closer to the set in order to hear.

To say Mule was an addition to my family of neighbors would

be an understatement. Mule added himself to my household much the way I imagined one's relatives did.

By now the winter months had seen their worst days, and spring neared. I longed to see these mountains and valleys in bloom, discover what variety of flowers grew at this high altitude.

While daydreaming about warmer weather and finishing up my morning chores, I heard Nakani's voice.

"Where is your respect?" she scolded. I could only guess she was scolding Mule. "I saw you making yourself annoying to Rooster yesterday. You are not so important! Just because you are so large, you don't forget, Rooster is your better!"

I dried saucers, bowls and plates, put them in the cupboard, wondered, with a grin on my face, what Mule was being chastised about. Within seconds, the story arrived.

"Mule has been stepping on Rooster's corn!" Nakani snapped and almost spit. She caught herself in time. I'd put a stop to her spitting in the house or car.

"Stepping on Rooster's corn? Why do you think that?"

"I have witnessed!"

I have witnessed, I thought, sounds like something a person ought to say after a baptismal ceremony. "What exactly was Mule doing?"

Nakani pulled out one of the dining room chairs and seated herself. Unlike Kopeki, who always sat on the floor, Nakani preferred comfort. "I'll have some coffee," she said.

Sure, why not? Only meant I had to brew some in my freshly washed coffee pot. "Coffee will take a few minutes," I said. "So what did Mule do?"

"Ben put some corn in the courtyard," she began, paused, narrowed her eyes and said, "Rooster's corn..."

"...and the Happy Hens," I added, talking to her through the kitchen doorway.

"And the Happy Hens...yes...but it's not for Mule! Mule is jealous. Soon as Ben put out the corn, here comes Mule. Then, what do you think he did?"

I shrugged, finished measuring water and grounds, set the brew switch.

"He trots into the courtyard and stomps the corn into the dirt!"

"He what?" I laughed.

"Into the dirt! Rooster and Happy Hens were not very happy about that."

Nakani's upset seemed out of proportion to Mule's crime. Still, there was one thing I was beginning to understand about Nakani's histrionics: she enjoyed the drama. I stood in the doorway with my arms crossed and asked, "Didn't they scratch it out? Chickens do that."

"Do what?"

"Scratch their food out of the dirt," I said. "That's a normal behavior for chickens."

"Mule is very jealous," she said, clucking her tongue.

I leaned across the kitchen sink, peered outside. I could just see the top of his back and head. Mule was standing close to the dining room window and his ears were bent forward. If I didn't know better, I could've believed he was eavesdropping on our conversation. I chuckled to myself. He was an interesting fellow. I could believe he enjoyed ruffling Nakani's feathers—or I should say, Rooster's.

After coffee Nakani said, "What are we going to do today?"

"We?"

"You and me. What are we going to do today?"

"I know what we aren't going to do."

"What's that?"

"We aren't going back to anymore ceramic stores. . .much as I would like to get started on a project. . .test that oven, see how well it bakes clay."

"What oven is this?"

"Don't mind me. I'm thinking out loud."

"Which oven would you use for clay?" she asked. She seemed genuinely surprised.

"One down by the pueblo ruins. I saw those three dome ovens; one's in pretty good shape. My guess is it's been kept up for use in the recent past. Sam said he didn't know who might've been taking care of it. Would you?"

Nakani shook her head. "Sometimes the ancestors come back to practice old ways. . .or teach them," she said.

I raised my eyes into a questioning expression, but Nakani was off on a new topic.

"Not very good clay," she said.

"What clay?"

"Clay at Popper's Peppy."

"Pepper's Pottery," I corrected. "Well, I don't know that much about clay. That's why I decided on ceramic slip. A lot easier." I frowned. "But it doesn't matter. Ceramic slip or clay. It's pointless. You got us thrown out of the place—thank you very much—and barred from ever going back."

"You're very welcome." Nakani got up and went to the window, pulled the drapes back, was met by Mule's large ear a few inches from the glass pane. "You act like the old men!" she yelled. Mule's ear twitched, but stayed where it was. She faced me, said, "They don't know where to find good clay. I know where to find it."

"You know a different store?"

"Best clay is at the river."

The river? I didn't say anything, I just waited for her to continue.

"Honda can get us there quickly," she said.

"Which river?"

"Mother River."

"I never heard of it."

"It is very near."

"The Rio Grande?"

"That's her."

"Will we need shovels and buckets?"

"Good idea," she said. "I will return when the sun is there," she pointed overhead, which I guessed meant about noon. "You be ready. Tell Honda to be ready."

I nodded. Why not? Maybe she was right and she knew where to find good pottery clay. After she left, I changed into my oldest jeans and ragged flannel shirt, and slipped mud boots over my canvas sneakers.

I was putting two shovels and two large buckets into the Honda when I heard Nakani returning.

"Lazy old man!" she called across the field to where Mule napped in the sun. If he heard her, he was ignoring her. I chuckled and shook my head, remembering how she and Sam had twisted my arm to let Mule stay. I'd come to believe she enjoyed arguing with Mule more than anything else she did; something she'd never admit.

I was surprised by her dress. Certainly not what I would wear to dig clay from a river bed. Her sack dress was bright yellow. Tied round her waist was a white apron lined with blue ribbon and decorated with woven figures of birds and stalks of corn. A brown blanket filled with large yellow butterflies was draped over her head and across her stout shoulders. She wore brown moccasins. On her head she balanced a beautiful pot that was painted with geometric bird shapes. In one of her hands she carried another beautiful pot. This one had painted deer dancing and running around its base.

"You dressed for a party?" I joked.

"The gathering of clay from Mother River is a sacred job."

"It's a dirty job."

She eyed my sloppy attire, clucked her tongue and said, "You magicians sure like your opposites."

"That we do," I agreed. By now I knew they believed I really was a magician, capable of flying away in the form of my true white hawk self anytime I chose.

I had to watch myself, not forget it was simply their magical mythical thinking. I was fond of the idea.

"What are the pots for?" I asked. Outside of a museum, I'd never seen more magnificent pottery. The one she carried was large enough to hold about a gallon of liquid. The clay was light beige, and the rim was encircled with two thin lines of black paint. The deer were black, with red arrows symbolizing a life line stretching from their mouths to their hearts. They had white patches on their rumps beneath their pointed little tails. They all had full antler racks, and the positions of their long stick legs showed they were busy, moving, continuously in motion. The pot balanced on Nakani's crown was of a similar color, but different in shape. It's fat body abruptly narrowed into a bottle neck top, and on each side it had coiled handles which arched, leaving holes barely large enough to slip one finger through. The bird figures were joined in the middle like siamese twins, but each had its own head, and exaggerated beak. A square bulls-eye design, combining black diagonal lines with strokes of red, decorated the birds' bellies.

"I am not a magician," she said. "Mother River expects me to bring gifts. I have corn pollen, and I have piñon nuts."

"Interesting," I said.

She narrowed her eyes and studied me, waiting for tricks, I guess. "Shovels and buckets are in the car," I said. "If you're ready, let's go find good clay."

We drove to a clearing alongside the ruddy, muddy Rio Grande at a place about eight miles from my home.

"We are near the good clay spot," Nakani said.

I parked the Honda and got the shovels and buckets. Nakani carried her pots. After locking the car, we began our trek up the river's bank. We walked easily when the bank was flat, but we occasionally had to hike over small hills and across rough arroyos. "I thought you said we were near good clay," I complained while we paused to rest at what I guessed was the two mile mark from where we'd left the Honda.

"Very near," she said, balancing the pollen pot and holding tight to the piñon nuts pot.

Though it was a pleasant crisp cool day, I gasped for breath; my clothes were soaked with sweat from the exercise. When I looked at Nakani, she was as fresh as when we'd left the house. Who is the magician here, I wondered.

Finally, at what I estimated was three miles from the Honda, Nakani exclaimed, "Good clay is everywhere now!"

"Where?" I asked, staring at the red river rolling by with a subtle roar.

"Everywhere." She went to the edge of the bank and tossed the contents from her pots into the water, then said, "You see?"

Following the direction she pointed to, I saw what she meant. There really was clay here. I was practically standing on it!

I stepped cautiously closer to the rolling waters, and raised my voice to be heard, "Where is it coming from?"

The clay mud was heavy and separated itself from the thick liquid Rio Grande by clinging in sticky clumps to the sides of the bed and bottoms of narrow inlets, which spread out like tree branches from the larger river.

"Mother River brings this good clay down from the sacred mountains when most of the snow is melted."

"So this is top soil off the Sangre de Cristo's," I mumbled to myself. I was kneeling, digging my fingers into it, enjoying the heavy, slippery consistency. "This is real clay," I said with a loud happy sigh.

"This time for Pus-chuts-otes is a good time to find this clay," Nakani grinned and winked.

"What time is that?"

She eyed me again with that "What is the magician up to?" look, and said, "Pus-chuts-otes is one word for the time of sticky ground. Another word is April. Kopeki calls this tH li'tekwakia thlan'na: the time for big wind moons. All the same. It's time to find best clay. Mother River brings this to us because the winter rains have been many. When the rains do not come, this clay cannot be found."

I gazed up at the enormous sky, looked out across the river, noted how the sunshine kissed the water with splashes of bright reflective radiance, and marveled at the approaching spring, the music of birds who puffed their breasts to sing their melodies out for all the forest to savor. I could have been in anyone's heaven. I could not have been happier. "Thank you, Mother River," I said. Suddenly I felt generous. I stood up, stretched my arms, yelled, "Thank you Mother Earth, thank you Sangre de Cristos, thank you blue sky, fresh air, and wonderful birds!"

Nakani was surprised by my outburst, and confused for a moment, then she followed my actions and repeated my words. When she finished, she turned to me and smiled.

"This is a special country," I said.

She nodded.

We both sat and looked at the world for awhile. And then, with Nakani's help and supervision, we filled one of the buckets to the rim with clay of a quality I didn't believe could be matched. I was ready to fill the second bucket with clay when Nakani said, "No. This is for sand."

"Why sand?"

"You have to mix sand with clay if you want to make nice pots."

"Okay," I said, glancing around, spotting some sand, digging my shovel in.

"That's not very good sand," Nakani said.

"What kind of sand are we looking for?"

"Soft sand. . . soft like new babies."

I shrugged, handed her the empty bucket. She started walking up the river bank with her shovel and bucket. I followed. We hiked at least another mile before she stopped at the base of a rock cliff where a small white sand dune had formed. She knelt and used her fingers to sift first one area, then another. Next she used her hands to scoop down into the dune, continuing to sift all the while. Suddenly she sat back on her heels and said, "This is very good sand."

I hurried over and knelt beside to watch what she did. She removed a fine soft piece of cloth from a pocket in her dress and tied it across the top of the bucket, thus beginning a painfully slow process of sifting sand, one handful at a time, through the cloth.

The sun was in the western sky, indicating it was late afternoon, before we made it back to the place where we'd left our clay and Nakani's two pots. We decided who would carry what, and were almost to the Honda when Nakani set her load on the ground and started up a shallow arroyo carrying only the shovel.

"Where are you going?"

"We will need painting tools," she said.

I waited and watched while she went over to a tall stringy plant and began digging around its base. Eventually she had the part she wanted: one spindly leaf. Using the shovel, she broke it at the root line and brought it back to where she'd left her load. She gathered everything, including the yucca leaf, and we completed our journey back to the Honda.

17

Nakani sat on the steps at my back door and worked the yucca down to its blade, tearing off strips, chewing the ends, and spitting the scraps, until she had two sturdy brushes.

"They're a lot like quills," I said.

"What are quills?"

"Feathers," I explained, "prepared similarly. People used to write with quills. I imagine some people still do."

"I can make brushes with feathers, too," she said, "but this is better."

I picked up the yucca brushes and rolled them over and over between my fingers, said, "These would be difficult to improve on, I have to agree."

Nakani nodded, then got up and went into the kitchen, returned with my largest mixing bowl and a pitcher of water. She resumed her place on the steps, pulled the buckets close to her feet and plucked out some of the clay. By now it was dry and powdery. She sprinkled it with some of the sand, dropped this in the bowl and added water, kneading the mixture with her hands, alternately adding clumps of clay with sprinkles of sand until it became a medium sized ball. She held it up for me to admire. I touched it, noted its fine silky consistency.

"We will leave this now," she said, rinsing her hands with what was left of the water and drying them on her skirt. She stood up and started to leave.

"Where should I put it?" I asked, pointing to bowl and clay.

"It isn't going anywhere," she said.

"I know that. But should I cover it and put it in the refrigerator to keep it moist?"

She shook her head, then left. I stood there for a short time, wondered what to do with the clay left in the first bucket, and the sand left in the second. Then I lifted the ball of clay from the mixing bowl and rolled it in my hands for a few minutes. I didn't know much about clay, but I could sense something about this clay. It was about as perfect as clay could get, making me curious about where Nakani learned these skills. I knew if I asked her she'd reply, "From my ancestors."

I never did ask.

Next morning while finishing my shower, I heard the living room door open, but it didn't close. I hurried to dry myself and pull on fresh jeans and sweatshirt, assuming it was Nakani.

"There is no more coffee," Kopeki's voice called through the closed bathroom door. "This is very disappointing," he added.

"See what's on television," I called back, patting my hair dry while combing out tangles. "I'll make you a new pot."

I heard him sigh happily. A few seconds later I could also hear that Kopeki was playing with the remote control again.

I made his coffee, then joined him in front of the television. He had settled for an old repeat of "I Love Lucy," which I'd discovered was his favorite—aside from Saturday morning cartoons' sneaky coyote and speedy roadrunner.

"Lucy is a very good Kosh'airi," he said, turning to notice me during one of the many commercial breaks. "I think Lucy is probably a master Kosh'airi. No, I think Lucy is probably the supreme Kosh'airi."

I sipped coffee and nodded.

At that moment Lucy and Ethel appeared on the screen. They were plotting some bit of mischief when Ricky came into the room. Lucy immediately went into an act designed to trick Ricky into giving her money for a new dress.

Kopeki laughed, "Lucy is a very good Kosh'airi."

"I believe I've seen this one," I said. "Ricky gets wise to her scheme in the end."

"Ah," he said, "White-Hawk woman is a jealous magician."

I was trying to think up a clever response when Nakani walked in from the dining room.

"Today you will learn to make good pottery," she said to me, ignoring Kopeki.

I left Kopeki with his red haired Kosh'airi and followed Nakani to the back steps. "It's cold out this morning," I said. "Why don't we take this stuff to the workshop?" I gestured at the small building I'd already decided to use for ceramics.

Nakani nodded. She picked up the bowl with the ball of clay, stuck the yucca brushes in her hair, and walked to the workshop. I went into the house to get the key for the lock, and when I came out, I saw she was already in the workshop. Why be surprised? I stepped into my dining room, dropped the key into my handbag, went back outside, picked up the buckets of sand and clay, and joined her.

She was sitting on an upturned tree log, leaning over one of the work tables. I brought another log in, positioned it as she had, and sat across from her. At first she pressed the ball with her fingers, then she tore a piece off, rolled it between her palms, then placed it on the table and patted it as flat as a pancake.

"This begins my pot," she said. "Now, you begin your pot."

I tore a chunk of clay off the larger ball and patted it into a similar shape.

Next, she tore off another piece and worked it between her hands the way bakers worked bread dough. "Make sure you get out all the air," she instructed.

I took more clay and copied what she did. When she was satisfied her piece was bubble free, she rolled it between her palms to make a coil. I did the same. She placed her coil around her pancake base, and made more coils. As the coils created the shape of a bowl, she would pat and rub, and smooth them out, tapering the bowl's sides. It looked so easy. It wasn't easy. I copied every move she made, and still my bowl was lopsided and dented. Her bowl was beautifully shaped, round and slick as glass.

When she stopped working the clay and stood up to admire her pot, I asked, "What now?"

"The clay will sleep now. When the sun is there," she pointed at the sky in the area where the sun would be around ten o'clock, "I will be back."

I said nothing. She was obviously as much a master at making pottery as Lucy was at playing the clownish Kosh'airi. When she was gone, I sat and marveled at her clay pot. And then my eyes were drawn down, to the floor, to the two buckets.

I ran to the house, poured a pitcher full of water, and raced back to the workshop. The bowl was empty. We'd used all the clay Nakani made the day before to create our pots. I grabbed the bowl, pulled it closer, and positioned the buckets at my feet. With nervous trembling fingers I plucked bits of clay, dropped these into the bowl, added sprinkles of sand, and drops of water. Gradually I worked this mixture with my hands until it felt like moist satin under my sensitive finger pads. I continued doing this until I had a ball about the size Nakani had made. I wanted to work with it then. Right then. I wanted to try making another pot. I wanted to make pots until I could make one that looked like hers.

"Better let the clay rest," Kopeki called from the workshop doorway.

His voice surprised me and I spun around, unbalanced my log, and fell off. While I was gathering myself together and getting up, Kopeki said, "This was a good fall, but not so great. Lucy can make a great fall. She is. . ."

". . .a supreme Kosh'airi," I interrupted and finished his sentence for him. He only grinned. "Kopeki," I said, "Why is it important to let the clay rest? Couldn't I mold it like it is? It seems firm enough."

He closed his eyes and shook his head. Then he looked up and said, "Pot making is for patient people. I don't think you will ever be a good pot maker, White-Hawk woman. I think you would be a better warrior hunter. I wonder if you will ever decide what you want to be?" He paused and mused over some thought in his mind. I waited. Then he said, "Maybe when you were created, somebody forgot to finish you. Maybe you will always be halfway between what you're supposed to be."

I didn't follow him at all, as usual. "Right now I'd like to make a nice bowl," I said, staring at Nakani's creation.

"Well, you still have to let the clay rest. Good clay cannot be hurried. It wants to sleep. After the sun sleeps again, you can make your bowl."

Kopeki had his fill of morning television, and had finished off the pot of coffee, was getting ready to leave, when Sam drove into the yard.

"Big auction over at Española today!" Sam said excitedly as he slid down from the GMC's cab.

"Sounds pretty good," Kopeki said.

"Wanna go?"

"Let's go," Kopeki said, hurrying to climb into the truck.

"Wait a minute," I protested. "What about me?"

Sam was crawling behind the steering wheel, and Kopeki was sitting in the passenger seat with the window down, his arm resting on the door. "What's that?" Sam asked.

"What's so exciting about an auction?"

Sam cast a quick look at Kopeki. Neither one said anything.

"Why don't you invite Nakani and Ben, and those other friends of yours . . . the ones that went with us to San Felipe . . . and why don't you ask me if I'd like to go to an auction, too?"

Sam looked at Kopeki again, then he stuck his head out the window, "You wouldn't be interested in this auction."

"Really? What's being sold off?"

"Rugs," Kopeki said.

I stared at Kopeki. "How'd you know?" I was getting suspicious. "I didn't hear Sam say anything about what kind of auction was at Española. He simply said there was a big auction today."

"Lot's of good rug makers over in that area," Kopeki said.

I knew something was up. I pretended to lose interest. "Just a rug auction," I yawned. "Well, I've got to clean my workshop. Have a good time."

Sam turned the truck around, but slowed to a stop near where I stood. "If Nakani comes 'round," he said, "don't mention the rug auction."

"She won't be back today," I said. I fought back my curiosity, maintained a bored expression.

As soon as they were down the driveway, I raced to the house, grabbed my handbag and keys, and jumped into the Honda. I followed at a good distance, all the way to Española. Sam parked the GMC across from what looked like an old school building. The parking lot was crowded with old cars and trucks, new cars and trucks, and a few horses were tethered to a nearby chain-link fence. I waited until Sam and Kopeki were into the building before I found an inconspicuous place to park the Honda.

When I entered the building, hand-printed signs directed me to a gymnasium-sized room packed with people. A man stood on a platform in front of the room and pointed a long stick at a huge rug which hung from a gigantic frame.

"Who'll gimme fifteen? who'll go fifteen? who'll go fifteen . . . ," he asked, his words repeated in rapid succession. A hand went up in the crowd, and the auctioneer carried on with the bidding until the rug was sold for twenty-two thousand dollars. I gasped at the idea of paying so much money for a rug. But as soon as that one sold, another one went up on the frame and the bidding started all over.

I inched my way into the room and moved cautiously through the crowd, careful not to let Sam or Kopeki see me before I saw them.

There they were: my two ancient fossilized friends, sitting in the back of the room with a group of elderly women. I moved closer, but kept myself hidden by the crowd. A man standing next to me whispered, "You come to these auctions often?"

I shook my head.

He whispered, "Didn't think I'd seen you around before."

"Where do they get all these rugs?" I whispered.

The man gestured to the back of the room, "Those old Navajo women are rug makers," he whispered. "They each make about one of these a year. Bring them in for the auction. Money they make off one rug carries them to the next auction."

Navajo? No wonder they didn't want me to tell Nakani. She'd have a fit if she knew her husband was here flirting and gossiping with a bunch of Navajos. I couldn't hold back my amusement, and had to cup my hand over my mouth to muffle my laughter.

"Better be careful," the man whispered. "The auctioneer will think you're bidding."

I thanked him, and made my way out of the room as quietly as I'd slipped in.

18

Next morning about ten Nakani walked through my dining room and stood in the kitchen doorway, waiting for me to finish washing up my breakfast dishes. Her silent presence was unusual. Usually she entered the house with her mouth in motion. I wondered if she'd guessed what Kopeki and Sam had been up to the day before. I held my silence as well. None of my business what those old fossils did.

When the last dish was dried and put away, we walked quietly to the workshop. She stood for a few minutes and studied her bowl, then she turned her attention to mine. "You need a lot of practice," she said.

I grinned, glad she'd finally broke our spell of silence. "I need more than practice," I said, "I need a miracle."

She faced me, asked, "Why does a White-Hawk woman want to make pottery?"

"Makes me feel good...like I can create something with my hands, something pretty," I said.

She frowned. I knew she didn't believe me. I doubted I could give her any reason that she'd be satisfied with, and we both knew it hardly mattered. I was going to learn to make a decent bowl if I had to dig up half the river's clay, sift a mountain of sand, and chew yucca leaves till I puked.

Nakani was holding my warped-excuse-for-a-bowl, running her fingers over its dents. "The walls of your pot are too thin," she said.

I picked up the bowl she'd made, put my index finger inside, placed my thumb pad on the outside opposite where my finger was. Gently I turned the bowl around, keeping my finger pads on its walls, tried to sense the thickness. Nakani watched me, understood what I was doing. She handed me my bowl. I did the same with it. Now the difference became obvious. It was slight, but I could feel it. She was right.

"I've made more clay," I said. She looked into the mixing bowl, went to it, picked up the ball, pressed it between her palms.

"This might be good," she said. I accepted the compliment.

"There's enough. . . we can both make a new bowl."

She shook her head. "I am going to make paint."

"Out of what?"

"I have this," she said, pulling a small black cake of something that resembled chewing tobacco from her pocket.

"What's that?"

"I used this before," she said, "a very long time ago. It is dry. I will need a metate so I can make it ready."

"But what is it?"

"It is the juice from a plant. Some call it guaco. You must find the leaves before they are too dry and you put them in a bowl with some water and put it on the fire."

"What's a metate?"

"Metate is for grinding grains. A very fine stone."

"I don't have a metate."

"I can find one," she said.

I watched her walk down to the pueblo ruins. A short time passed and she returned with a large flat rock and a smaller round stone. She put the large one on the floor then knelt before it, placing the dry cake on the metate. Using the smaller stone, she began to grind the cake until it was a powdery black flour. I went to my kitchen, found an oven proof dish, and carried it to Nakani. She brushed the powder into the dish and added water.

"I will put this on the fire," she said, carrying the dish towards the back door.

"You'll have to build one," I called. "The hearth is cold."

"A hearth should never be cold," she called back, her tone scolding.

Chuckling to myself, I wondered if she meant that philosophically, decided I understood her too well. She meant the hearth shouldn't be allowed to get cold. Period.

After positioning my log-filling-in-as-a-chair until it was somewhat comfortable, I sat at the table and studied Nakani's bowl. I ran my fingers over all its surface, closed my eyes and tried to sense its lines, its shape, its character. While doing this I could sense this bowl possessed its own energy. At first I thought I imagined it, but when I opened my eyes and looked at it, the energy was there, watching me. I set it down abruptly, then picked it up again in a panic. I rolled it over in my hands, my heart racing. Luck was with me! It wasn't cracked.

"Geeze," I gasped, glancing back at the doorway. Mule was there, peeking his large head through the opening. "Think what Nakani would do to me if I broke this," I whispered. He stretched his neck and shook his head. I laughed, "You understand, don't you?" He snorted.

I carried her bowl to the empty counter in the far corner, gingerly placed it next to the wall, out of harm's way. "There," I said. Mule snorted again.

I scooted the mixing bowl down my worktable, sat on my log, and looked at the clay I'd made. I plucked a small piece off the ball and patted it until it resembled a three inch tortilla. I plucked another piece and rolled it into a coil. Carefully, I positioned the coil around the tortilla base. I rolled another coil, placed it on the first coil. Repeating this action, I worked until I had a four inch stack of coils. Now what to do. The coils needed to be smoothed together. Resting my elbows on the table, groaning, and pulling at my earlobes wasn't getting the job done.

But! I had an idea. I hurried to the house, got a small container from my cupboard, and poked my head into the living room to see how Nakani was coming with her potion. "Is it paint, yet?" I asked.

"Yes," she said. "Why? What else would it be?" Suddenly she spun around on the hearth and said, "Don't you turn it into something else! I have spent much time with this paint!"

"It's just a figure of speech," I said.

"And you are just a magician," she said, raising her voice.

"Don't get upset about nothing."

"Trickster," she said with a cluck of her tongue. "Go away and let me finish this paint. . . and don't turn it into something else!"

Nakani was a case. As I was turning to leave, I heard her spit into the burning coals. At least she wasn't still spitting on the floor. I cringed. Not exactly a nut-case, but she was a case of some kind. I wasn't sure there was a name for it, or even a category for her. I wasn't sure there was a category for any of my neighbors.

When I got to the workshop, Mule was busy scraping the side of his head up and down the doorjamb, scratching his ear. "What do you think that ought to be?" I asked, patting his neck and pointing at my pile of coiled clay. He stopped scratching his ear and focused his big brown eyes on my project. "Maybe a cup," I suggested. He snorted. "Okay," I said, "it's a cup."

I set the container on the table, poured in some water, and added a few pinches of the fine satin sand. Using my finger, I stirred the mixture to create a milky liquid. Now I dipped all my fingers into this, coated them, and began smoothing the coils.

When the mixture became too liquid, I added more sand. I continued this until all the surfaces were silky smooth. Then I closed my eyes and tried to sense thickness. Too thick. I dipped and rubbed, and dipped and rubbed, and checked again. This felt right. Now for the handle. Plucking off a small piece from the ball, I pressed and formed it with my fingers to make a thick flat strip. Working the top end carefully, I sealed it to the side just under the rim, arched it out to allow room for two fingers to pass under, then sealed the bottom end just above the base.

I stood up and backed away from the table to get a better view of my creation. "Well," I said to Mule, "what do you think?" He yawned and closed his eyes.

"Be rude," I said. "I really don't care." He pretended to be instantly fast asleep. I scratched his big ears and slid out between his bulky shoulder and the doorjamb, returned to the house. Nakani was using her skirt hem to lift the hot dish out of the coals and set it on the hearth.

The tar-black inky liquid in the dish smelled terrible. Actually, the entire house was filled with that smell. I threw up several windows and prayed the smell wouldn't linger in my furniture. "Can we paint with it while it's still boiling like this?" I asked.

"Psstpsstpsst," she hissed. "Where is your patience? You have forever to do anything." She threw her hands into the air and started out the back door towards the workshop. "Agh! Magicians!" I heard her spit on the ground.

I sat on the hearth and wondered what I was supposed to do with this dish full of malodorous ink. Leave it where it is, I thought. Nakani wasn't going to forget it. I joined her in the workshop.

"Where is Mule?" I asked, noticing his absence.

"I told him to go and annoy Rooster," she said.

I threw her a suspicious frown. Now she wanted him to annoy Rooster? This was the same woman who accused me of being a master of contradictions. Nakani was a walking contradiction. No wonder Kopeki sought out the company of a bunch of old Navajo women.

"Sit," she ordered.

I positioned my log across the table from her. She was already busy building another gorgeous piece of pottery.

"This is very good clay," she said, avoiding looking at me. I could see the corners of her mouth turning into a slight smile. I also noticed, she was using my sand and water mixture to dip her fingers while she worked her coils smooth. "I am thinking this White-Hawk woman is using magic, maybe?" She was stealing a few quick looks at my finished cup.

My turn to smile. Nakani was jealous! I plucked another chunk off the shrinking ball of prepared clay, began patting out a tortilla shaped base. Didn't matter to me if she believed the only way I could learn this art was by use of magic.

We spent the best part of the day using up the prepared clay. I made two more coffee mugs, carving a different name across the bottom of each. I planned to surprise Sam and Kopeki with cups. I also watched Nakani while she fashioned her projects into water jars, or tinajas, as she called them. Then I made my own tinaja, and was pleased when Nakani stopped working and followed me to the back counter, where I placed it next to her bowl. She stood at the counter and studied it for a very long time.

When all the clay had been transformed into objects, we cleaned the table and I washed out the buckets and containers.

"When can we put these in the oven?" I asked.

Nakani shook her head and grunted, "Ovens are for food."

"Then where are we going to fire our clay?"

She eyed me curiously, as if she believed I really didn't know how to fire pottery. In the absence of a professional kiln, she was right. I didn't.

Saying her words slowly, she explained, "When the wind is resting and the sun is generous, we will make a fire and bake the pottery. If the wind is busy, smoke will get on the pottery. It will be ruined. A good place to make the fire is here," she pointed to the side of my yard, near the dining room window.

"Why here?"

"We have to watch the fire, keep the coals hot, until the pottery is done. Best to have the fire here."

I shrugged. It was all an educational learning experience for me, and I was enjoying it thoroughly—even if Nakani did believe I cheated and used magic.

That afternoon, while Nakani was leaving in the direction of the pueblo ruins, I decided to catch up and walk with her, find out once and for all where my neighbors lived.

At first I walked briskly, but she was always just far enough ahead not to hear when I called out for her to wait. When she had descended the hill, she did not stay in the courtyard. I began to run. Then, just as I rounded the courtyard wall, I saw her dropping into the hole that led into the passageway tunnel which ran beneath the pueblo. I raced to the tunnel, lowered myself down through the emergence hole, and stared at the shadows ahead which echoed only emptiness.

Nakani was gone. It was as if she disappeared. I crawled the length of the passageway. She wasn't there. I called out her name as loud as I could. No reply. I called for Ben, or Kopeki. Still no reply. I knelt near the hole, where sunlight allowed me to examine the dust on the ground. I could see my footprints, and my hand prints. I did not see anything else.

19

I crawled back and forth through the passage tunnel, eventually losing count of how many times I'd retraced my own steps. At first I guessed Nakani knew of another exit out, perhaps a short-cut to where ever it was she lived. But what kind of shortcut? The pueblo ruins butted into a rock cliff, and the tunnel seemed to run below the full width of the ruins, exiting into the ruins—and she wasn't there, either. I searched. Room to room. Room to corridor. Corridor to horse room, where I was met by Rooster and Mule. Rooster and Mule accompanied me out to the courtyard.

Outside all was quiet and still. Rooster and Mule seemed to sense my feeling of aloneness, and I was glad for their company. I scooped my hand into the feed sack, gave Mule a mouthful of corn and sprinkled kernels on the ground for Rooster, who was quickly joined by the Happy Hens. I sat on the cold earth next to the feed sack and mused over the tunnel's well-kept condition.

Who kept it up?

Why?

For what use?

Why no prints?

Nakani didn't leave any physical sign of having been there.

Some deep sense told me I understood this strange phenomena.

It was possible my ancestral memory understood.

My ancestors.

My neighbors.

Their ancestors.

People from this land.

Sometimes all unknowns are known.

I hiked up the stairway which led to the hilltop above the ruins and was making my way back to my house when I heard Sam's

GMC. I hastened my pace, and reached him before he was out of the cab.

"Afternoon, Missy," he greeted.

"Afternoon," I said. "Want to come in and share some lunch? I haven't eaten yet."

Sam looked up at the sky, said, "Past lunch time. My daughter-in-law fixed me some sandwiches 'fore I left home." He glanced in the direction I'd come. "You been over at the ruins?"

I nodded. I wasn't hungry anyway.

"Where's Mule?"

"He's at the ruins, visiting Rooster and the Happy Hens."

Sam grinned. "That Mule's a card, ain't he?"

"That he is. Of course, I'm afraid Ben didn't take to him like we thought."

Sam shook his head. "Well, that's the way it goes sometimes. Can't always make things turn out like we plan 'em, you know."

I shrugged, "Well, now," I said, "we didn't really plan the accident that brought Mule here in the first place, did we?"

He shook his head again.

"Hey," I said, remembering the clay, "you want to see my pottery?"

His eyes seemed suddenly alarmed. "You haven't been collectin' stuff from these here killin' grounds, I hope," he gasped.

"No, no. I know better than that." I winked and added, "Wouldn't want to offend any of the ancient ones."

"Wouldn't want to do that," he sighed with relief.

"Come on back to the workshop." I led the way, then stepped aside for him to enter the building.

"Well, looka here!" he exclaimed, smiling. "I didn't know you were a potter! Nakani'll be right surprised, she will."

"This is all Nakani's doing," I said. "Nakani had me drive her to the Rio Grande the other day. We dug up the clay, she found some sand, she got a yucca leaf to make brushes with, and she made her own paint. She also showed me how to combine the clay and sand to form pottery clay."

"You're kiddin'! She did all that? Now, I'd say that's a right big surprise. That Nakani don't take to many folks. She says it takes too much energy to spend time with most folks. She don't waste her energy, I can guarantee you that. Well, I don't think

Nakani ever wasted her energy tryin' to get to know my wife. Didn't give two spits for her."

Sam paused, gazed through the open doorway, across the hill country. I noticed how time had carved up his face, burrowed deep through his pale skin. I often wondered where he found his energy. Then I began thinking about years again: chronological years, and people's ages, and I was sure Nakani couldn't have been born while Sam's wife was still living, at least not when she was living here.

"Sam," I said, "Nakani is a very young woman."

"She does age good, don't she?"

I ignored his sidestepping. "How could your wife have known her?"

"I'll bet that Nakani's been tellin' fibs 'bout her real age," he grinned and winked. "She does get real sens'tive 'bout bein' older'n Kopeki."

Older than Kopeki, I thought. Poor Sam. But at least he had his moments of coherence. Sam went to the corner table, began picking up the dry pieces and bending close to get a better look at the fresh pieces. "This here bowl is mighty authentic," he said, touching the pot Nakani made with our first batch of clay.

"That's not mine," I said.

"No," he said. "No, I knew the bowl wasn't yours. But these here cups are darned good."

"Glad you like them. Which one's your favorite?"

He studied them, and finally said, "Hard to decide. Why?"

"One's yours. I made them for you and Kopeki, so you'll have your very own coffee mugs to keep at my house."

"Reminds me, it is a very good afternoon for a cup of coffee," Kopeki said, poking his head in the doorway.

Sam greeted the newcomer, showed him the pottery Nakani and I had been working on for the past few days. Kopeki grunted and muttered something in his native tongue which I couldn't understand.

"Kopeki says pot making is woman's work, and he isn't very interested in it," Sam translated.

I thought, Kopeki's saying this for Sam's benefit. I shrugged, "Guess Kopeki won't want one of these coffee mugs, then, will he?"

Sam winked, "Guess he won't."

Kopeki grunted again, then picked up the larger cup and said, "If I am forced to have one of these, I think you can make me take this one."

I glanced at Sam while speaking to Kopeki, "Oh, I wouldn't want to force you to own a piece of woman's pottery."

"I cannot offend the White Hawk woman," he said. "I will take this one. When will it be ready for me?"

"Nakani tells me we have to wait for a day without any wind," I explained, walking out of the workshop and gazing across the distant valleys. Early spring was owning up to its Zuni name: tH li'tekwakia thlan'na, or time of the big wind moon.

Kopeki and Sam followed me outside. Kopeki said, "Kwashi'amme is a good time to put pottery in the fire. Not much wind, then."

"When's that?"

"Kwashi'amme is the Zuni word for May," Sam said. "It means no name moon. I've heard Nakani refer to May as Showats-otes, meanin' the time of soft ground."

While we were trying to decide which month would bring us a day without wind, I spotted Mule plodding through the front yard. Mule saw us and changed course, plodded over to stand with his head between Sam and Kopeki.

Mule set his large soft muzzle on Kopeki's shoulder, his big ears seemed to droop. Kopeki was nodding and sighing, then he whispered something to Mule, turned to Sam and me and said, "Mule has been watching a memory, and now he is not happy."

Right, I thought, asking, "How do you know?"

Both old fossils fixed me with stern expressions. Sam said, "Why, that's what Mule here was sayin'. Said it real clear, didn't he, Kopeki?"

Kopeki said, "Real clear."

I asked, "Is this a joke?"

They didn't say a word, and their expressions remained stern. "What?" I asked. "You mean Mule can talk?"

Kopeki cast a quick glance at Sam, whispered, "This White Hawk woman might be up to some of her tricks."

I looked at the three of them, and they stared back. "Why would I be up to tricks?"

"Maybe you already decided to take Mule to visit his memory

place so he wouldn't be unhappy," Kopeki said. "Maybe you wanted to surprise him."

"Right," I laughed. "That's exactly what I wanted to do—give Mule a big surprise."

"Why, that's mighty generous of you," Sam said. "But how you figure'n on takin' him there?"

What was I getting myself into? "No, wait, I'm joking, really." Sam and Kopeki grinned and winked at me, and Sam whispered in my ear, "We get it. You want to keep it a surprise."

"What are we talking about?"

The men ignored me. Mule kept watching me. The men walked off toward Sam's GMC. Sam was pointing at a trailer hitch on the back of the truck. They stood there, discussing this surprise for Mule—I guessed—while I tried to imagine what was going on. When they finished their powwow, they started toward the house. Kopeki raised his voice and said, "It is still a good afternoon for a cup of coffee."

I left Mule to go make a pot of coffee. Sam and Kopeki sat in the living room enjoying their brew, gossiping about some past adventure they'd had when they went to a summer kachina ceremony at the Acoma pueblo. They spent the remainder of the afternoon comparing stories about journeys "up that rock."

Kopeki went home and Sam drove away, and I walked out to the yard, asked Mule, "What did you say to them?"

May arrived and I'd forgotten about Mule's surprise—which was easy since I never found out what it was.

One morning, while finishing my shower and getting dressed, I heard Sam's GMC pulling into the front yard. It sounded different, as if the engine were having to work harder. I hurried to slip my boots on, then opened my front door in time to see Mule's back side disappearing into a small horse trailer attached to the GMC.

"Where're you taking him?" I called out, running to the trailer.

"Ain't takin' him nowhere," Sam said. "This is so's you can give him that big surprise. I'm lettin' you take him."

"This joke is going too far," I argued.

Sam ignored my protests, continued, "Mule's been watchin' some of his memories, lately. Got himself right unhappy, he has. What you gotta understand is, before he got himself retired—now he don't like to think about his retirement, and that big truck that hit him, 'cause that upsets him . . ."

"What's going on, Sam?"

"That's what I'm gettin' at. Anyway, Mule used to have a pretty good job . . ."

"Mule had a job?"

"There you go, interruptin' me again!"

"Sorry."

"Mule got to haul folks up the Burro Trail over at Acoma— every year durin' the month of May. That was his job. Pretty good job, too. The rest of the year, Mule says he lived over near Pojoaque. But come May, he'd get hauled down to the sky city. That's what he calls Acoma. Right fittin' name. Sky city."

"Why only during May?"

"Cross Day's in May—it's a holiday—and them Acomans got this cross that sits up top of Burro Trail. Don't know why it's there. Maybe has somethin' to do with that Catholic fella, Father Ramírez . . ."

"Who was he?"

"You're interruptin'," Sam snapped. "I don't know who Ramírez was, except he was one of them Catholic fellas. Rumor is he had that Burro Trail built. Anyway, lotta folks like to ride donkeys and mules up the Burro Trail on Cross Day. When they get to the top, where that wooden cross sits, these folks put flowers on it."

"And you believe Mule misses that?"

Sam ignored me. "Here's the ignition key," he said. "Now you're prob'ly gonna need to wear a jacket. Can get right chilly out there if the wind gets up."

"Sam," I said, taking his shoulders in my hands and giving him a firm shake. "Sam, I don't know what you want me to do, and I have no idea where Acoma is."

"Acoma's easy to find. Once you get close, you can't miss it. Big old rock sittin' on a mesa. Shoots up off that mesa 'bout three hundred and fifty feet, or more. Top of the rock spreads out, seventy five acres. It's a big rock. Oldest inhabited pueblo in the country, that's Acoma." He paused and scratched his chin, gazed off in the direction of the ruins, then added, "Course, we ain't countin' Kwapoge, here. Our Kwapoge ain't got no more ho'i."

I followed his gaze, and thought a minute before I asked, "Is that the lost pueblo?" I pointed towards the ruins.

He winked, "That's our Kwapoge."

I'd read about a lost pueblo called Kwapoge. It was supposed to be somewhere north of Santa Fe, and it was supposed to be very ancient. I searched my memory, tried to recall what ho'i meant. It was one of Kopeki's words. Then I remembered. A live person. Ho'i was the Zuni word meaning 'a live person.'

20

My ancestors weren't from southwestern soils, but they were like my neighbors: native to the soils of America. Maybe that's why I let my neighbors take over my home and interrupt so many of my days. Maybe that's why I willingly allowed them to virtually invade every aspect of my life.

In an abstract sense, they were relatives, and I enjoyed them. But Sam was my favorite, although he wasn't family, and he wasn't an actual neighbor.

Mule was also a favorite. Sam and Mule were near as I'd gotten to ever having best friends. I'd never wanted a best friend before. Never wanted anyone or anything that close to me. Not my adoptive parents, not the people I went to school with, or worked with, or lived next door to.

I'd always been a lonely person. Not because I was alone. I was usually surrounded by people, and I had more than my share of men cluttering up my life, trying to break my heart. Never worked. You have to care about someone before they can break your heart.

Maybe that's why I was here. I often thought about these changes in me. Often wondered if it was part of some Great Spirit's Master Plan. Often tried to imagine what that plan could be.

While I pondered over these esoteric philosophies, Mule napped in the horse trailer, which I was towing behind Sam's GMC. I'd already been on the road for three hours, and by the map, it looked like I had another hour to go. Acoma was slightly less than sixty miles west of Albuquerque. Forty five of those were easy miles on Interstate 40. The remaining fifteen would be less friendly after I exited at Casa Blanca to head south.

I had no idea how long this venture was going to take, and

guessed we wouldn't get home until late. Sam borrowed my
Honda and drove himself to Santa Fe. He said he'd bring
the Honda back and pick up his truck in a day or two. I told him
the Honda was full of gasoline, and he wouldn't need to stop for
any. He told me the GMC was getting close to empty, and I
would need to stop.

That damned GMC's tank took sixty dollars to fill. I planned
on remembering that when Sam brought my Honda home.

When I reached the Casa Blanca exit, I pulled the truck onto
the shoulder to check on Mule. This entire adventure was for him
and I imagined he was awake now, growing more excited the
closer we got to Burro Trail.

Wrong. He was sound asleep. I slapped his rump, yelled,
"Mule!" He inhaled a deep breath of air, exhaled, and continued
to sleep. I crawled in the cab, shifted into first, and got back on
the highway.

My philosophical mood began to fade, and an attitude more familiar emerged. I cursed and beat my fist on the steering wheel,
wondered what person in their right mind would be doing this?
How did I let those two old fossils talk me into spending a day
hauling Mule out to a rock in the desert?

I was approaching the point of talking myself into swinging the
truck around and heading home, when I saw it. "Oh my god!" I
gasped and eased off the accelerator, coasted to a stop at the side
of the road. It lay there like a huge gray dinosaur resting on the
mesa.

I couldn't believe I hadn't been more curious about this im-
pregnable, beautiful, mysterious rock. I stared at it through the
windshield until I lost track of how long I'd been sitting there.
Suddenly Mule kicked the side of the horse trailer, brought me
out of my trance.

I drove the rest of the way in first gear, too spellbound to remember to shift. I parked the GMC off Main Road, near the
Camino Del Padre Trail. Now Mule was awake, and eager to get
out of the trailer. For the first time I noticed a large riding saddle,
a saddle blanket, and a halter with reins in the trailer, laying on
the floor in the empty stall beside where Mule had been.

"What am I supposed to do with these?" I asked myself. Then
it occurred to me, I couldn't just turn Mule loose, tell him to have
a good trip up Burro Trail. I would have to ride him. I didn't

have a clue how to put the saddle on. I did manage to get the halter on, because I'd watched Sam with it before.

Luckily, there were quite a few people passing. Most walked, but some rode horses, and all were carrying flowers. I guessed they were celebrating Cross Day, which meant they were going up Burro Trail, too. I stopped a middle aged Spanish couple, asked them if they'd help me with the saddle. The man crawled down from his horse, threw the blanket across Mule, swung the saddle over the blanket, and cinched the belt which stretched under Mule's belly. I thanked him, and they left. I'm sure they wondered how I was going to ride up a steep and difficult trail, when I couldn't even manage the saddle. I was wondering that myself.

Mule snorted and shook his big head impatiently. "Glad you're raring to go," I said sarcastically. "Hope you had a nice nap, because you better be damned alert. How the hell do I get myself into these messes?"

Mule stretched his thick neck around to get a better look at Sam's saddle. He nuzzled the stirrups, tried to pick up the scent of the horse or mule who last used it. I took the reins and led Mule up and down the trails at the rock's base, trying to build courage to climb on the saddle and begin our ascent.

Trouble was, the more I stalled, the less nerve I had. Walls of white rock towered above me, casting afternoon shadows which engulfed me each time I passed under overhanging cliffs and slabs of stone. Mule's restless snorting increased, and I was tiring of passers-by staring. "Damned the torpedoes and full speed ahead!" I yelled, reaching for the pommel and pulling myself up on the saddle. Mule stretched his neck again, eyed me curiously with a big brown peeper, and I said, "What're you staring at?"

Several people hiked by on foot. They threw quick glances, and gave me plenty of room. "Mule used to work this route," I said to them. "He knows what we're doing." They hurried off up the trail. "Okay, big fella. Let's go."

Mule started at a quick walk. We passed between two large rocks and traveled a very short distance before we arrived at Burro Trail. Mule really did know this place. We began our ascent, and he placed each sure-footed hoof carefully, but confidently, as if he could make this trip with his eyes closed. I held tight to the saddle pommel, and pretended not to be afraid I would fall off and tumble down that stone dinosaur.

In no time we caught up with the foot-hikers who stared rudely earlier. "I told you," I called out, "mule used to work this route." Mule closed in on them, they stepped aside, and we were off and climbing.

Mule did the work; I feasted on my surroundings. Mostly our ascent was steep and dizzying, and several times I saw where big stones had been positioned to create rude platforms. Once we passed directly beneath a dislodged boulder—huge enough to crush us both—held in place only because it was trapped between narrow cliff jaws.

Evergreen shrubbery clung in sparse patches, seemingly sprouting from the hard stone. This shrubbery spotted the rock with specks of color more frequently as we neared the top.

Then, when we were about fifty yards from the cross, Mule stopped. At first I couldn't understand why we didn't continue. But while we waited in the shadows of a slender stone column, I heard a noise. Looking up, I saw half a dozen people kneeling before the cross. A priest stood over them while they prayed. When they raised their heads, the priest blessed them.

Three more people on horseback rode up behind Mule. They glanced up the trail, reined their mounts in, and we all kept our silence, waiting in the shadows of the stone, until the people at the cross disappeared behind the summit of Burro Trail.

Mule allowed a few seconds, then he closed the distance to the cross. The three riders followed. At the summit, Mule paused while I studied the huge wooden cross, observed all the fresh flowers placed on it, around it, and nearby.

The riders dismounted and were kneeling to pray. I felt embarrassed and awkward, like an intruder, and wondered if I should dismount and pray with them. But I'd never prayed to a wooden cross . . .

Mule walked wide around the cross, solved my dilemma. We were off on a new adventure, which took us first to the outside edges of Acoma Pueblo. A huge adobe church perched atop a shallow hill. At the front, two towers braced its face, extended skyward, maybe twenty feet. One tower had large open windows, and housed a bell. The opposite tower had small windows. It seemed more of a watchtower than a belltower. Each tower was crowned with a white wooden cross, as was the center of the church's face. The face had one window high above the single doorway, and I thought how it resembled a mud Cyclops. Surrounding the church was a mud and stone fence, and before it, enclosed by part of the fence, was a huge graveyard—two hundred feet square in size, I estimated.

I dismounted and looped the reins across Mule's neck so he wouldn't step on them. "You wanna take a closer look?" I asked him. "If you don't, just stay here and graze," I gestured at the dry grass carpeting the ground. "If you're game, follow me."

When I reached the church, a priest was standing in the shadow of the watchtower. "Buenas tardes," he greeted.

I smiled, "It is a very good afternoon. Thank you."

"I recognize your animal," he said, staring at Mule. "I didn't know what'd become of him. I heard his owner passed away last year. The family took the animal out to the old killing grounds near Pojoaque and let him go. Least that's what I heard." The priest turned his attention to me. "How'd you come by him?"

"He was trying to get across the highway near where I live— which isn't too near Pojoaque," I said. "Another mule went across first, and a truck hit him. Killed him—the other one, that is. A friend witnessed the accident and brought this one to me. No one's been by to claim him, so I let him stay."

The priest sighed. "Wonder where the other one came from? Maybe they were both orphans left to wander alone. Probably decided to wander around together."

"I guess," I shrugged. "I've gotten very attached to this one. Felt real bad about the one that died."

Mule fixed his big brown eyes on me and tilted his ears toward us. I could believe he understood our conversation. The priest reached up and patted Mule's nose. "I've been seeing this animal here same time every year for about fifteen years," he said. "Always someone different riding him. He's a smart one. Hauls people up the Burro Trail, then takes them on a tour of the village. Afterwards, he hauls them back down the rock. I imagine his owner made a lot of money off those rides."

"Oh," I said, "I'm sure he did. But I'll bet Mule enjoyed his job more than his owner enjoyed the rental money."

The priest laughed. "His job? Yes, I see what you mean. Would you like to visit our church while you're getting your tour of the village?" He glanced at Mule. "I'm sure your guide won't mind. By the way, I am Father Stephen."

"My name is Dana Whitehawk," I said. He smiled politely and turned, and I followed him through the doorway, into the church.

The floor was bare, and I thought of San Felipe, remembered what Sam said about the reason there weren't seats: it was an Indian church. I guessed there was a distance of about forty feet from ceiling to floor. The walls were a bare off-white, except for a design painted in red. The design looked like a small repeating circle and it ran the length of the wall. Behind the altar was a crude painting, divided into six separate full-length portraits of kings and saints—I guessed. Looking down at these, another painting near the ceiling showed a facsimile of a Catholic Christ.

The priest noticed me staring at the paintings. "Not very good artists," he said. "It was completed by some Mexicans about 1802. Do you see the painting on the left?"

I nodded.

"That one is much better. King Charles II of Spain loaned that to the Mission. I hope he didn't expect it back."

We both laughed. I couldn't remember what year King Charles II reigned, but I knew it was a different century. The scene depicted a bearded man dressed in a long green gown with a white cape. He held a trumpet like thing in his right hand, and he cradled a child in his left arm. The child seemed to have the face of a man. I had no idea who they were, or what the scene was about.

"It is one of the miracle-working paintings," Father Stephen said. I pretended to understand.

"Do you know the history of our church?" he asked.

"No," I said, hoping this wasn't going to be like one of Sam's stories; I'd be here until dark.

"Actually, the history of the church rightfully begins with the history of Acoma."

I held my breath. This was going to be a long story.

"Acoma gets its name from Akome, meaning 'people of the white rock.' Acomans have a myth that even today, some believe. It's about a group of people searching the world for a place their kachinas called Ako. Because they are pueblo people, they always have twins for everything," he said, pausing to see if I understood.

I nodded, said, "Like opposites."

"Yes. Like opposites. These twins were called Masewi and Oyoyewi. Every day they led their people, and called out 'a-a-a-k-o-o-o,' until they finally arrived in a valley and heard their calls echoing. They looked up and saw this big white rock. They found a way to the top, and this is how the Acomans came to be here. According to the myth."

"That is very interesting," I said, wondering what time it was getting to be.

"Captain Hernando de Alvarado was the first non-Indian to see it. Alvarado was with the expedition group of Coronado in 1540. Later, around 1600, Juan de Oñate sent Don Juan de Zaldívar up here with about three dozen soldiers. Unfortunately, the Acomans thought he was their enemy and they killed him, along with a dozen of his best soldiers." The priest paused to bless the four hundred and fifty year old victims.

I thought, the Spaniards were their enemies. The priest signed himself with the cross and started up again. "Oñate was a determined man. He sent Zaldívar's brother, Vicente, with about eighty soldiers. They managed to get up here, and they put fire to the village. Six hundred Acomans died, and six hundred were captured. . ."

I thought, now why doesn't that sound fair? The Spaniards lost thirteen people, so they killed six hundred and imprisoned another six hundred to avenge their dead.

The priest was still talking, ". . . and after they threw one hundred of the prisoners off the rock, they marched the remaining five hundred—mostly children and women—to Santo Domingo, where they were allowed to work for the church and king. . ."

I interrupted, asked, "So why do they have a Spanish church up here? Seems to me the last thing I'd want, if I were an Acoman, would be a Spanish church."

"Well, well," he said cheerfully. "You haven't heard of Father Ramírez."

"Didn't he have something to do with Burro Trail?"

"Oh, yes," Father Stephen said. "Father Ramírez was quite the visionary. He dreamed of building this very church. But he needed to get the materials up the rock, so he built El Camino del Padre. . ."

"The path of the father," I translated.

"The Path of the Father," he repeated. "And, of course, Burro

Trail was built next. Some materials were too heavy for the Indians to carry, so they used burros."

"Of course," I said.

"Construction was difficult, and took many years," he said. "The Indians had to bring these vigas," he pointed at the logs in the ceiling, "from the Cebolleta Mountains."

"Where are they?"

"About thirty miles south of here. This wonderful house of God," he stretched his hands toward the ceiling, "was dedicated to Acoma's first patron saint, Saint Stephen. No relation. And it was given the name, San Estevan Rey."

"That is all very interesting," I said. "Would you know what time it is?"

He checked his wristwatch, said, "Four o'clock. I don't give my next services for several hours." Then he looked up at me and asked, "Will you be staying for services?"

"I'd better go find Mule and get started down the trail," I said.

"Oh, but I haven't told you the whole story of our church."

"Really?" I believed I'd heard all I wanted to hear. I thanked him for his kindness, and his generous story-telling, and started walking out to the courtyard.

"Have you heard about Pope?" he asked. I remembered the story Sam told me about Pope, and the great Pueblo Rebellion.

"Yes," I said.

"Did you know the Acomans took their village back and killed their priest, Olasqueain? They reverted to their pagan ways until 1700, when Spain once again ruled all Pueblo people."

"Well, gee," I said, "isn't that interesting?"

He was keeping pace with me while I searched for Mule. "Did you notice our graveyard?" he asked.

I nodded.

"Forty years," he said. "Took forty years to build it. Notice the frame that surrounds it? That's forty feet deep in some places. To fill it, all the dirt had to be hauled up from the mesas."

"You should write a book about this church," I said. Just then I spotted Mule. "Mule!" I yelled. He perked up his ears, then trotted to meet me beside the outer fence wall. I hurried to climb up on his saddle.

"Are you sure you won't stay for evening services?"

"We have a four hour drive ahead of us," I said, "and we'd better get started down Burro Trail before the shadows make it dangerous for Mule." Father Stephen extended a hand for me to shake, and I reached down to accept his gesture of friendship. "Thank you for spending so much time telling me all about San Estevan Rey," I said.

"You're very welcome," he said. As Mule was turning toward Burro Trail, he called out, "Are you Navajo?"

"No," I called back, and then I said more softly, "I'm just a mixed-up brand of ketchup."

Mule began to gallop, and I imagined Father Stephen returned to his church to prepare for evening services with his Acoma parishioners. I wondered if he ever told them their history.

21

Mule and I underestimated evening traffic through Albuquerque. It was bad enough I was hauling a trailer and driving a full size pickup, making myself easy target for anyone practicing rude driving habits, but I wasn't very good at either. Hauling a trailer, or driving a truck.

We ended up in the Marriott's parking lot waiting for traffic to lighten. I pulled around to the back of the hotel, let Mule out, and sat on a concrete curb. Mule wanted to sample the hotel's manicured lawn, but I persuaded him to wait till we got home and I'd give him some of Rooster's corn.

Why the Marriott parking lot? Why not. It was between an easy-off exit and an easy-on freeway ramp. The hotel's manager disagreed.

"Lady, what the hell are you doing?" the short bald man asked, approaching me, Mule, and the truck-with-trailer as quickly as his stubby legs could move.

"I'm resting," I said.

"Not here," he insisted.

"What're you going to do about it?"

"You're distracting some of my better customers."

"How's that?"

He gestured wildly at Mule, who studied him with wide curious peepers.

"Your customers never seen a Mule?"

"This is a respectable establishment."

"We aren't doing anything disrespectful," I said. Mule dropped his head until his nose touched my shoulder. I reached up and scratched his chin.

"I'll have to ask you to move."

"I'll do better than that. I'll be gone completely. But not till that lets up." I pointed at the nearby freeway, dense with vehicles.

His round little face turned red. "Can you at least move to another parking lot?"

"No."

Needless to say, he didn't convince me to move. Mule and I remained until nine p.m. But before I loaded Mule, I led him to the restaurant service door, asked one of the employees for a bucket. "What's it for?" the young boy asked.

"Mule is thirsty."

The boy poked his head out the door, Mule struck a pathetic pose, and the boy carried a bucket of water to him. I thanked him, Mule snorted, and we left the Marriott.

I'd maintained a steady cruising speed of fifty during the daylight. The closer I got to Santa Fe, the slower I had to drive. And by the time we were climbing north of Santa Fe, my speedometer didn't exceed forty. No more trailer hauling for me. I couldn't unhitch this thing, and I was damned sure not going to drive it again.

Next morning, before making coffee or taking a shower, I did what I'd done every morning for weeks. I hurried outside and stood between the house and workshop, held a feather at arms length, and checked the wind.

"It is resting," Nakani's voice called from the workshop. I went to look inside. She was assembling all our finished pieces on the table nearest the door. She turned to look at me, noticed my nightgown, wrinkled her nose. "That is a very ugly dress."

"It's not a dress," I said, speaking rapidly. "Now, don't start the fire without me. Wait, okay? I'll be right back. Don't start the fire without me, okay?" I spun around to leave, but was halted by a thought, "What about the paint? I thought we were going to paint some of our pieces?"

"I painted yesterday," she snapped, "it is too late for you to paint. Where are you going?"

"Give me five minutes," I said, racing back to the house. I jumped in the shower, lathered, rinsed, and pulled sweater and jeans over my wet body. Too late. By the time I was outside, Nakani was laying cedar bark on the ground near the side of the house. She handed me one of the buckets that we'd used for sand.

"Go find more of this," she said, holding up a piece of bark.
"And find some dry branches."

"Cedar branches?"

"Bark and branches should be from the same trees."

"Okay," I said, leaving to roam the hillsides. Most of the trees
on my property were cedar or piñon pine, making bark and
branches plentiful. I filled the bucket, took it to Nakani; she separated the bark, tossed it on the other bark, and set the branches
aside.

"You will need to find plenty more," she said, handing me the
empty bucket. Like a small child obeying orders, I returned to the
hillside and filled the bucket until Nakani said, "Enough! Let's
bring the pottery."

While we carried our pieces to the prepared site, I thought how
much I'd mellowed these past months. It was nothing short of a
miracle. I chuckled quietly, remembering why I'd selected this
particular house: isolation; solitude; no neighbors. But here I was,
willingly letting these strange souls into my life. I had to laugh
aloud at that. What choice had they given? Locked doors and
windows didn't keep them out of my home, and my coffee bill
had quadrupled. Not to mention the feed bill...

It occurred to me, at this rate, I'd have to go back to work
pretty soon. Doing what?

"You are a pretty good potter," Nakani said. She was kneeling
beside our pottery firebed. "I am sure you could learn to be a
master potter."

A master potter? As in, a paid potter? Now there was an
idea...

"Don't fly away with the clouds," she scolded, noticing I was
daydreaming. I knelt beside her, watched how she stacked the
heavier clay pieces on the bottom layer of bark. She kept generous
spaces between each piece...

"To let the clay cook," she explained, again reading my
thoughts.

That is when I noticed she'd decorated all my pieces, as well as
her own. The old Dana would've had a fit. An angry screaming
fit. This Dana only shrugged and sighed, thought her friend, Nakani, was a very good artist.

Now Nakani was busy building a bark blanket over the first
layer of pottery. I scooped up some bark, helped with this new

firebed. When it suited her, she carefully placed all the best pieces on this layer, and built a final cover shelter with more cedar bark. She stood and examined this unusual mound, clucked her tongue, and hurried to the workshop, retrieved the other bucket. She practically ran past me, saying, "Let's go. Bring your bucket."

What now? I picked up my bucket and followed her across my property, down the pueblo stairway, into the ruins, to the horse room. She started scooping up horse droppings.

"What are you doing?" I asked, shocked.

"Fill your bucket," she ordered.

I filled my bucket with the old dry manure. When we both had our quotas, she trotted up the hill, me a few yards behind. At the house, she kneeled before the firing mound, took a small leather pouch from her pocket, dipped her fingers in and removed pinches of corn pollen. She sprinkled this on the mound and prayed for good pottery.

To my surprise she built yet another layer of cedar bark, and finally she covered the entire thing with dry, flammable, horse dung.

"You can put the fire on," she said.

I dug a book of matches out of my jeans pocket, struck one, and touched it to the dung. The flame took hold immediately, and soon we were watching our pottery cook.

The mound burned with a steady clean flame. It was too hot to get near, but Nakani and I watched it for hours, adding more cedar bark and branches to spots where the coals died down. "We have to make it burn the same all over," she said.

And we did. We kept heat evenly distributed through the mound, and several times Nakani commented, "It is a good bake. All the pottery will be good."

"I wanted to do my own painting," I said, my tone was not upset or scolding. It was simply a statement. "I wish you'd told me you were going to paint yesterday."

She looked up, her eyes asked, "Where were you?"

"Sam and Kopeki convinced me Mule wanted to visit a memory. Seems Mule misses his job climbing up Burro Trail over at Acoma." After the words came out, I wondered if I was beginning to believe any of this.

"Why did you go?"

"I had to haul Mule," I explained, nodding my head towards

the GMC, which was parked in front of my house with the horse trailer hitched behind.

Nakani glanced up at the truck and trailer. "Mule doesn't need that," she said.

"How else would he get there?"

She clucked her tongue and spit on the fire. "I believe Mule has tricked our trickster," she said with a half grin, adding, "Mule can travel anywhere he wishes to go, just like the wind." She snapped her fingers loudly. Then she lifted her attention to the heavens and her eyes seemed to focus on a large cloud which moved slowly in the still sky overhead. With a quiet sigh she whispered, "I do not understand why this White-Hawk woman believes she must have strange kachinas," she gestured at the GMC, "to take her where she wants to go. I think this White-Hawk woman was snatched from her own oven too soon. I am sure she is not done."

I leaned on my heels and watched her, suddenly remembering how she disappeared into the tunnel beneath the ruins. Then I thought about what Father Stephen had said about Mule's owner being from Pojoaque. Sam and Kopeki insisted Mule told them he was from Pojoaque. My mind recreated the scene on the highway. I closed my eyes, got a good look at the dead mule. I shook the idea out of my mind, opened my eyes, and tossed another handful of bark on the fire.

When all our bark and tree branches were used, Nakani said, "We can go and watch television now."

"What about our pottery?"

"When white ashes are all that is left, our pottery will be done. Even then, we will have to give the pottery time. It will be very hot. If we take it too soon from the ashes, it will break." She seemed to be studying me while she said this, and I knew she was comparing me to one of those pots.

"Okay, fine," I said. I'd resigned myself to obeying she-who-insisted-on-being-obeyed, and we left our fire to burn itself out, retired to the living room—where Kopeki and Ben watched yet another ancient repeat of "I Love Lucy." Kopeki was comfortable in his usual spot on the floor near the hearth, and Ben was in the best chair.

Ben turned briefly to say, "I have brought a basket of eggs. I put them in your cold box."

136

"Thank you, Ben," I said.

I sat on my sofa and counted the seconds it took for Kopeki to say, "It is a good day for a cup of coffee."

Twenty seconds.

The afternoon was late when we all went out to look at the fire. The dung had long burned away and the coals were now white ash. Ben kneeled and touched a finger first to his mouth, then to the ash. "It is ready," he said to Nakani.

Nakani searched the yard, found a stick, and used it to scatter the ashes and dig out each piece. She sat them in a row between us. So far things were looking good. Her bowls were gorgeous, and I admired the designs she used to decorate the sides: continuous geometric lines circled each piece, growing thicker at the bases and rims. I remembered the potsherd I'd once found in the ruins. This was a similar design. When she removed the tinajas I noticed she'd painted the one I made with a large bird of prey. I guessed it was a hawk.

Finally she got to the coffee cups. The first one she plucked out had my name on the base. She'd painted little rabbits jumping around its perimeter. I didn't comment, but the rabbits were surprisingly cute and comical. Rabbits to feed the hawk, I guessed. The next was Kopeki's. She'd painted a facsimile of my coffee pot on this.

"Ah, this is my favorite picture," Kopeki said to Nakani.

"Don't forget," I reminded him, "I made the cup."

"Thank you very much for this gift," he said to me, his smile stretched until his teeth showed.

Last in the fire was Sam's cup. She dug around with the stick and had trouble finding it. When she lifted it out and sat it beside me, I saw a huge crack running through it.

"It's broken," I groaned. I bent closer to look at the little frogs Nakani had carefully painted on Sam's cup.

"Frogs are for good luck," Nakani assured me.

"I guess there weren't enough of them," I joked.

Nakani and Kopeki exchanged somber looks. Ben said, "Will Sam come to live with us, now?"

"Why would he do that?" I asked.

Ben said, "It has been broken here, on the killing grounds." He looked at Kopeki and asked, "Since it is broken here, won't he have to come?"

Kopeki said, "I think it is a good day to go for a walk in the Sacred Mountains."

With that my neighbors left me standing alone with the cold fire and all the pottery. Suddenly a swift breeze dipped out of the heavens, stirred the still air and played havoc with the white ash.

22

My neighbors didn't return that day.

Or the next day.

After raking the ground to clear away the firebed, I carefully carried each piece of pottery to my dining room, displayed them on the table, and spent a great deal of time sitting, staring blankly at the pottery.

Mostly I stared at nothing.

I could sense the changes. Changes in me. Nakani was right. I was like clay. I was like an unfinished project. A piece not baked long enough, taken too soon from its fire.

I wondered about my birth parents.

Not important.

I wondered about sisters or brothers.

Not important. Sure there were none. Couldn't be more than one like me. The idea made me laugh. My laughter seemed to feed itself, and I couldn't stop. I laughed, and laughed, and then I was crying.

Mule must've heard. He was pressing a concerned nose against the window pane, smudging the clean clear glass with slobber made green with chewed grass. I wiped the crying off my face and reached out, touched his nose through the transparency. "We are very similar," I said. "You and me. You were left to wander like an orphan. I'm glad you found me. I think I've always been wandering. Never felt connected. Sometimes forcibly tied. Not connected.

"Mule, you and Sam are my best friends. Pretty strange, huh? You. A big ugly animal. Sam. An ancient old fossil whose days are already borrowed. What a set of friends. Don't think it was my idea. Choosing you guys for friends. I mean, you can't choose your neighbors, but . . . What would I do without you guys? Huh?"

Mule snorted, blew sprays of green spit across the glass. I
stood, picked up Sam's broken cup. "I'll make him another one.
No more clay. Mule, I've got to go find more. I know how to find
it. Nakani taught me. She's really not bad. She does get on my
nerves. . .and I guess she tests you to the limits, but I think she
means well. You know?"

I glanced at Mule. He looked skeptical. "Really, Mule, I believe she does mean well. You know? Why do I keep saying that.
Sam says that all the time. Gets on my nerves, almost as much as
Nakani. He'll say something, then punctuate with 'you know'—
like I'm supposed to know? Why am I supposed to know anything that spills out of his ancient brain? You know? There! I said
it again. Why do I keep saying that?

"Hey, you want to go for a walk?"

Mule snorted again. By now the window was not transparent.
It was murky green. My fingers tightened around the broken cup
while I opened the door, stepped out into the daylight. "Look at
this," I said, holding the cup next to Mule's head.

Mule checked it out.

"See all those frogs? Nakani said frogs mean good luck. So why
did this crack? I mean, why this one? Everything else turned out
beautifully. Even my bowl! I made a horrible bowl. The walls
were too thin. Nakani said they were. Why didn't it crack? Why
didn't one of her pieces crack? Huh?"

I turned the cup around in my hands. "Look at all those frogs.
Jumping around. Looking like Happy Hoppers."

I sighed, "Okay, so it's just a cup. Why're we making such a
big thing out of it? Hey, what about our walk?"

Mule followed a few steps behind and we hiked across the hillside,
down the steps to the ruins. The courtyard was empty. I called for
Rooster and the Happy Hens, waited for Rooster to crook his colorful head around one of the broken walls. He didn't. "Where do
you think they are?" I asked Mule. It was too nice a day for them
to be roosting. I checked the first room, dipped my hand in the
feed bag, gave Mule a handful of corn. I poked my head into the
horse room. They weren't there. We left the ruins and searched
the area.

"This is strange," I said. Mule seemed uninterested.

"What if a coyote, or a wolf, or a mountain lion ate them?"

Mule snorted, shook his big head. Green spit splattered across my arm, across my white sweater.

"Great," I grumbled. "Look what you did. Do you think this will come out?"

Mule stretched his neck around, pretended to be interested in a covey of quail that appeared in the grass near a thicket of brush.

I seemed to be starting the day on a bad note. Where was the new Dana? The maturing, mellow, getting-smoothed-around-the-edges Dana? I didn't want to be grouchy, but I couldn't pull my attitude out of the gray spaces. I decided what I needed was to get busy. What I wanted was more clay. I could drive to the Rio Grande, where Nakani and I had gone. I could hike up the banks...

Wait! Drive what? I threw my hands into the air, yelled, "And where is my Honda? Sam! You promised to bring it back by yesterday!"

When we hiked back to my house, Mule led the way. My mood was dragging, and I imagined my chin was down around my toes. I stopped beside Sam's truck. I really did like the thing, and had begun to enjoy driving it. But not when it was attached to that horse trailer.

Suddenly it occurred to me I would have to go to Santa Fe and get my car. With Mule peering over my shoulder, I knelt to examine the trailer hitch, make sure it was secure, and was struck by how much it reminded me of an umbilical cord.

The truck.

The trailer.

Their inseparable situation.

Too bad the truck didn't have a gigantic pair of scissors.

I thought about Los Angeles.

I thought about my day of liberation.

"Okay, truck," I said, "I'm going to liberate you." I stood and faced Mule. "Sorry, buddy. You can't go."

I arrived in Santa Fe before noon. Pulling a horse trailer through town wasn't as bad as pulling it through extremely narrow residential streets, where unsuspecting people had parked shiny new Mercedes and Porsches and Lincolns next to the curbs in front of their homes. I shifted down—the GMC growled deeper with each lower gear—and snaked through the carefully swept, prim and proper upper-upper class neighborhood.

When I parked curbside before Sam Junior's hacienda, I saw my Honda parked in the driveway.

I rang the doorbell. Waited. Rang again. I used the doorknocker. And then I used my fists. No one answered.

My car was locked tight and I didn't have an extra key. "Damnit!" I screamed. I went back to the front door and gave another go with the bell, the knocker, and both fists. I considered going to the back door, remembered this was a hacienda. There was no back door. Besides this door, the only doors I'd seen opened out into the center garden, and that was walled in by the rooms of the main house.

"Sam!" I screamed, "What's going on?"

I looked up and down the street, decided to try some of Sam Junior's neighbors.

It was the same thing. No one was home. I didn't have much of a choice but to drive the thing home. Unless I could hot wire my Honda. No. Couldn't do that. I didn't know how.

I cursed until I used up my English vocabulary of good cuss words; then I cursed in Spanish; then I crawled into the truck and headed home.

Mule was standing near my driveway entrance when I turned off the county road. He kicked up his heels and ran, bucking, across the field at the far side of my house. I'd never seen Mule act like this before.

I accelerated quickly into the yard, shut off the ignition, and jumped from the truck, ran after him.

That's when I first noticed the pahos.

Hundreds of pahos.

My house was surrounded by prayer sticks.

Had Ben put them here? Why?

What was going on?

23

On the fourth day I was desperate. I hadn't seen my neighbors since the day we fired our pottery. Rooster and the Happy Hens were missing, Sam hadn't returned my Honda, and Mule turned antisocial. My big ugly friend didn't smear my windows with green grass spit, or follow me around the yard. He even refused to walk with me when I visited the ruins. All Mule wanted to do was stand in the front yard gazing off towards the Sangre de Cristos.

Twice I carried buckets of corn up the hill from the ruins. He ignored it. It might as well have been dirt.

Then I saw the car. With its speed reduced to a crawl, it eased down the county road and stopped briefly at my driveway entrance. I walked to the edge of my yard, watched it.

I heard the transmission shift from neutral to first. The car started moving again, rounded the fence, crept across the cattle guard, was getting closer each moment. I rested my hands on my hips, raised my chin, waited.

It was a polished white Cadillac sedan. The Cadillac came to a stop a few feet from where I stood and the driver crawled out, leaned against the door.

"First time I've been up here since I helped Dad move out," he said.

"Where's Sam?"

"Thought you'd want to know," he said, "that's why I came."

"Know what?"

"Funeral will be this afternoon."

I felt suddenly very cold, and it seemed I was having difficulty breathing. "Funeral? Whose funeral?"

"Sorry about this," he said, walking across the drive to where

Sam's GMC was parked, the trailer still attached. He placed a hand on its hood. "Dad loved this damned truck."

"Whose funeral?"

"Dad rented this horse trailer," he said. "I had to pay the owner a hefty penalty when Dad didn't get it back on time...plus I'm having to pay for every day it's out..."

"Whose funeral?"

He started to say something else. I didn't want his small talk cluttering up my head. "Whose funeral?" I screamed, running at him, pushing him away from Sam's truck.

He withdrew his arm quickly and stepped aside. I moved between him and the GMC.

"You're in the will," he said. "Guess I shouldn't tell you that since it hasn't been read, yet. But I've seen it. Thought you might like to know. The truck's yours. You'll have to take the trailer back to the rental agency. Maybe you can come by the house and get your car...soon. You can rent a tow-bar, tow it back here with Dad's truck...your truck."

A large shadow loomed over me, startled me, then a heavy muzzle rested gently on my shoulder. My arm seemed to be made of lead, it was suddenly so heavy. I strained to lift it, managed to touch Mule's soft nose.

"When did Sam die?" I heard my voice ask. Ridiculous question. Why was my voice asking a question when I didn't want an answer? Sam was my best friend. My very first friend...

Sam Junior shuffled his feet over the ground, used his expensive leather loafers to scar the dirt. He kicked at a pebble and said, "Four days ago."

I wasn't ready for this. "We haven't been to the Green Corn Dance," I said. "Sam says it's in August. We're all going...even Nakani. Sam says it's one of the best..."

"My father died four days ago," he repeated.

I raised my voice, "Four days ago we fired the pottery. I made him a coffee cup. Nakani painted it with frogs. She said the frogs were for good luck..."

"Who's Nakani?" he asked.

I stared at him, said, "She named you...I think...why are we having this conversation? My head is hurting...why are you here?"

He took a step towards me and I shrank back.

"You look pale," he said. "Maybe you should go inside, sit down . . ."

"No!" I shouted. I wanted to stand there and wait for Sam. He was supposed to bring my Honda back. Any minute he'd pull into my driveway. He would.

I whispered, "He's too old to die. Sam's a fossil. Too old to die. He's my best friend."

Sam Junior's face softened, and I could tell he was feeling sorry for me. I detested him and I detested his pity.

"I didn't know you were so fond of Dad," he said.

I stiffened my posture and tensed my muscles, but still my eyes filled with tears. It was too painful. I hated it. Having a friend. A best friend. Losing the friend . . .

"Will you be okay?" he asked.

"Where are my neighbors?"

He looked all around. "What neighbors?"

"They should be coming soon," I said. "Almost time for Kopeki's favorite program. I'll have to make coffee."

"I think you're in shock," he said.

I wanted to make him disappear. Nakani would've told me to zap him. Would that work? I wanted my head to stop hurting. "My chest feels very tight," I said. "I'm having trouble breathing. I'd like you to leave."

He took several steps away from me, said, "I had no idea you and Dad were such good friends . . . He spent so much time driving all over the country. I told him he was too old for that nonsense. Tried to get him to sell that truck . . ."

"He was taking the neighbors to see their kachinas," I said, surprised Sam Junior didn't approve.

"There aren't any neighbors out here," he insisted.

"Sam told me I'd like them," I said. "I do like them. I like them very much."

Sam Junior's face grew quizzical, but skeptical. I just wanted him to leave. I wanted to sort this thing out in my mind.

This emptiness.

Sam's fault.

He sold me this place.

Shared his neighbors.

Brought Mule.

Made me care about him.

And them.

I didn't like this emptiness. It was easier before I came here. Before I met Sam.

"I've always been a private person," I heard myself confess. "It's very safe, being a private person. No one gets close. No one really matters. . ."

"Funeral will be at four," he interrupted. "Saint Barnabus Cemetery. I need to get back to Santa Fe. I hope you'll be okay."

I walked to the house. Mule followed me. A short while after I went inside, I heard Sam Junior engage his ignition and drive his Cadillac away.

It wasn't a cold day, but I felt overcome by a chill. It settled in my bones and eventually penetrated my soul. I went to the hearth, built a fire, tried to warm myself.

Then I remembered what Sam Junior said. Four o'clock. Saint Barnabus Cemetery.

I stripped myself naked, ran a tub of very hot water, and bathed with the amole suds Ben kept in a bowl beside my bath. After my cleansing, I dressed in a long black skirt and a black silk blouse, wrapped my shoulders in a black shawl, and tried to clear my head.

24

During the memorial services I sat in the back of the church, listened without comprehension when the priest spoke Latin. I'm sure it was a good speech, but I wondered who it was delivered to? My eyes roamed the faces of the people in attendance. They couldn't understand Latin, either. I could tell. Their blank eyes stared ahead into the nothingness of confusion.

When the priest finished demonstrating his fluid command of Latin, people began to stand. Some wiped teary eyes. I spotted Sam Junior and Mrs. Sam Junior. They looked at me, through me, didn't see me.

Maybe they didn't want to.

Thought I was a case.

Like the neighbors.

Were the neighbors a case?

No.

Yes. I'd heard they were.

From who?

Me. I was the one I heard it from.

Changes in me were slipping away. It was too difficult. I'd valued privacy, the peace of solitude, until I came here and met Sam, was invaded by the neighbors.

Why had they forced me to change? At first I'd disliked their intrusions, tried to lock my doors and windows against them. They came anyway. Just like Sam.

I'd give it all back to them. Sam's house, his property. They could keep their killing grounds, their pueblo ruins, their prayer sticks and pottery and eggs!

Let them buy corn at a premium price for Rooster and the Happy Hens. And Mule. I'd find out where they went when they left my house, take Mule to live with them, make them buy his alfalfa . . .

Mule was my friend. I'd lose him if he went to live at their house. I'd lose my friend.

I hated this empty feeling. Preferred to be like I was.

Before these damned people made me care about them!

I thought, they've attached themselves to me. I hate attachments. I want to be free of them.

I liberated myself from Los Angeles, from the places and things that clung to me like a fungus. I liberated myself from that feeling of being smothered. It felt good, my liberation.

This was different. My head ached. My chest was tight. There was something wrong with my throat. Knots in my throat.

"You going to the cemetery?" a man's voice asked.

I looked out from my misery, noticed the church was empty. The people left me there, alone. I faced the owner of the voice.

He stood there, alongside the pew, looking very different than he looked in his uniform. I remembered how he'd looked that first time I met him.

"You ever get New Mexico plates for your car?" he asked.

"You have to wait long with that dead mule?" I asked.

One side of his mouth turned up in a half smile, made his thin black mustache crooked. "Had to radio for one of my deputies," he said. "Sheriffs ain't got time to wait around with dead animals. Too much important stuff to take care of."

"Like figuring out how a witch uses raw eggs to make a pachuco wreck his car and kill himself?"

Both sides of his mouth turned up this time and I noticed how much he resembled the actor who'd played Zorro. I couldn't remember the actor's name, but he was very handsome.

"Aye-yi-yi," he groaned, slapped a hand to his thigh. "You understand Spanish pretty good?"

I nodded.

"You eavesdropped on me," he said. "That's not very polite."

"You're a superstitious bastard," I said, feeling suddenly angry because I'd found myself attracted to him. I didn't want more attachments. Too painful . . .

"Usted tiene razón," he agreed. "Por favor, forgive me. What can I do? I am sorry."

"Why're you here?"

"Came to say adiós to old man Hoskins."

"You didn't like him. You thought he was crazy."

"He never made trouble for me," he said, spreading his arms. "Never made trouble for anybody. Thinking somebody's a little loco ain't the same as not caring anything about 'em."

"He's probably in the ground by now," I said, brushing past Sheriff Zorro, looking through the church's open doorway at the cemetery across the road.

"We can wait till the crowd goes," he said. "Sometimes it's easier to bid adiós to an amigo without a bunch of people watching."

I shot an angry look at him, "Sam wasn't your friend."

"Aye, but Señor Hoskins was your amigo."

I breathed slowly, felt the tightness gripping my chest. I stepped out of the church, stood in the late afternoon shade of the steeple, watched while people left the cemetery in small groups and pairs. Sheriff Zorro came to stand next to me. He was so close I could smell the fragrance of soap lingering on his skin. I wondered if he ever bathed with amole.

"You have a name?" I asked.

He seemed surprised. "Larry Tawayesva," he answered.

"Larry Tawayesva," I repeated. "Doesn't sound Spanish." I was thinking of Nakani. Nakani would never allow a Spanish Sheriff Zorro down the driveway.

He laughed. "I got family over at San Ildefonso Pueblo," he said. "Maybe some Spanish blood in there, somewhere. Who can tell? People around here don't worry about things like that so much anymore, Dana Whitehawk. Where were you from, before you were from California?"

I was amazed he remembered my name. "No where in particular," I said, not sure I wanted to invest more time in this conversation.

"Looks like the cemetery is empty," he said, glancing across the street. "You want to go alone?"

Alone? Sure. I wanted to go alone. Preferred it that way. He seemed to hear my thoughts. He glanced to the parking lot, said, "Guess I'll see you around, then?"

"Sure," I said. I started toward the cemetery, sensed an overwhelming emptiness. It was too late. I had been changed. My best friend was dead, and I was hurting so very, very much.

I heard myself call out, "Wait!"

Larry Tawayesva met me by the three-foot adobe fence surrounding the cemetery. He placed a strong gentle hand on my
shoulder and together we approached the fresh grave site.

"Look," he said, pointing at the ground.

The top layer of soil over Sam's grave was busy with the prints
of chicken's feet.

"Probably one of the old timers did it," Larry said.

"Looks like chickens did it," I said, thinking of Rooster and the
Happy Hens. But how would they get all the way down here?

"There's a few old timers who still believe in the ancient tradi-
tions," Larry explained. "Use to be, long time ago, when a person died, roadrunners were chased back and forth over the grave.
The people did this to confuse witches so they wouldn't know
which way the dead person's soul traveled during its hi'anyi."

"What's a hi'anyi?"

"That's the road the person's soul has to go on for four days. If
the witches get to the person before he reaches his happy land, he
ends up in a place like hell. I'm surprised whoever made these
tracks isn't sitting around puffing on cigarettes, blowing smoke in
the air. They did that to confuse the witches, too."

I tried to imagine Rooster smoking a cigarette. "You believe in
this?" I asked, remembering how convinced he'd been that I was
some kind of witch, that I played a role in Luján's accident.

He laughed nervously, replied, "Sometimes."

Suddenly, I realized Sam was in there, under all that dirt. Sam
the fossil, my old ancient buddy. I'd never see him again. I tried
to hold the tears. Didn't want Sheriff Zorro to see how vulnerable
I felt.

He was looking at me. "Want a handkerchief?"

I shook my head.

"Good thing," he said, digging in his slacks pocket, "I forgot to
bring one."

I knelt beside Sam's grave, closed my eyes. Larry thought I
was praying. I was asking Sam to be kind in his memories of me.
I apologized for calling him a fossil, for screaming obscenities in
Sam Junior's yard after finding my car locked up. I especially
hoped he would forgive me for not believing most of the things
he'd told me. Things about the neighbors, about Mule and the
dead mule, about how Nakani was older than Kopeki.

My head was still hurting, and my chest felt so tight. "I can't seem to get rid of this knot in my throat," I said to Larry while I got off my knees and brushed loose soil from my skirt.

"You could just let it out," he said.

My eyes raised to meet his.

"Woman," he said, his voice gentle, "you put up a big show being tough. My guess is you are pretty tough, but it ain't a crime to have a good cry. If this old man meant as much to me as he meant to you, I'd sit right there," he pointed at Sam's grave, "and bawl like a baby."

"It's getting late," I said, glancing across the cemetery to where the GMC was parked, trailer still attached.

"That yours?" he asked, allowing me to sidestep.

"Not the trailer. I've got to figure out where to leave it. It's a rental." I could tell he was dying of curiosity, but he resisted, waited for me to explain. I didn't.

"Address where it came from should be stenciled on the bumper," he volunteered.

Larry started for the parking lot. I knelt one last time beside Sam's grave and said, "Espero que nos encontremos otra vez, amigo." It meant, I hoped I'd see him again.

Larry Tawayesva offered to drive the GMC and trailer to the agency whose address was on the bumper. He gave me the keys to his vehicle, a beat-up blue Ford pickup. I followed in his Ford. When we reached the rental agency he said, "I can tow your car home for you."

I wondered what the catch was. "Why would you do that?"

He shrugged, "I'm not working tonight."

Did I want another person in my life? I wasn't sure. Maybe not. People didn't always stay around. I hated the way losing a person made me feel.

"Look," he said, "I'm not proposing marriage." His mouth turned up on one side again with a half smile. He was extremely handsome. And I didn't believe I'd ever figure out how to hook the tow-bar to my Honda.

"You remember where I live?" I asked.

"You think I'd ever forget?" he laughed.

25

I drove Sheriff Zorro's blue Ford, and he followed in the GMC with my Honda in tow.

Several cars passed him, got between us on the highway. I would have pulled over and waited, but he knew where I was going.

I just wanted to get home, make sure Mule was still there. I wondered if Rooster and the Happy Hens would ever return to the ruins. I wondered if my neighbors would want to visit, now that Sam was gone. I dreamed of another bath in amole suds. I wanted to build a fire and sit quietly in my favorite chair. I hoped if I did all these things, my head would stop hurting, my chest would relax, and the knot in my throat would go away.

As I neared the turnoff to my house, I tried to imagine what it would be like if I got to know Larry Tawayesva better. Maybe it wasn't a good idea.

Commitments.

Getting close to people.

Getting hurt . . .

The sun had dropped very low on the western horizon, but the world was still awake, and I could see Mule standing on the hilltop above the ruins. I parked Larry's truck near the front door, yelled, "Mule! I'm home!" He looked up, but stayed where he was. I thought he'd be curious about the Ford. He didn't seemed to notice it.

I was too exhausted to go check, see what his interest was in the ruins at this hour. I went into my house, collapsed in my chair . . .

"Where were you?" a man's voice scolded.

"I was busy with Rooster," another man's voice said. "I had to keep telling him, 'run across one more time.' He does not mind very well."

"You should have brought some cigarettes, blew smoke around in different directions. Why didn't anybody do the smoke?"

I jumped out of my chair, raced to the doorway, threw it wide.

Kopeki and Sam were walking across the hillside, Mule followed a few feet behind.

"I would have blowed smoke for you," Sam argued.

"I told you, Rooster needed a bunch of close watching. Didn't you like all the tracks he made?"

"SAM!" I screamed, running toward the three of them.

"What?" Sam asked, alarmed. "Is something wrong?"

"Sam?" I asked, slowing, stopping, reaching out to touch him.

"What is it, Missy?"

"We buried you today."

"That's right," he said.

Kopeki raised his eyebrows to me and said, "It is a very good day for a cup of coffee."

Gone was the pain in my head, the tightness in my chest, the knot in my throat. "Yes!" I laughed, "Yes, it is a very good day for a cup of coffee!"

The three of us started for the house and Mule followed.

Just then I saw Larry Tawayesva and the GMC with my Honda in tow, turning off the county road into the driveway.

Sam and Kopeki exchanged winks. Sam said, "I always said a girl pretty as our Dana here wouldn't be lonely for too long."